"You just left. And kept Luke a secret."

Emma swallowed hard. "I meant to tell you. I meant to before I went into labor. I meant to that first Christmas, his first birthday, every holiday and birthday after that. I have a shoebox full of letters I wrote you, talking about Luke and how he was growing up, pages filled with me trying to explain, trying to say I was sorry." She shook her head. "I should have told you."

Heartbeats passed, gave space for his thoughts, the emotions he couldn't begin to identify that were swirling around inside him. "You told me now, though. You came here now."

"I did."

"Why?"

"Because I knew I could count on you. Someone is after me. If something happens to me...I need to know Luke is safe and taken care of. I get that what I did, keeping him from you, is unforgivable. So while I'd love to have your forgiveness, I'm not asking for it. All I want from you is for you to help me keep my son safe. And if I can't take care of him anymore, if something happens to me—"

"I'm not going to let it."

Sarah Varland lives near the mountains in Alaska, where she loves writing, hiking, kayaking and spending time with her family. She's happily married to her college sweetheart, John, and is the mom of two active and adorable boys, Joshua and Timothy, as well as another baby in heaven. Sarah has been writing almost since she could hold a pencil and especially loves writing romantic suspense, where she gets to combine her love for happily-ever-afters, inspired by her own, with her love for suspense, inspired by her dad, who has spent a career in law enforcement. You can find Sarah online through her blog, espressoinalatteworld.blogspot.com.

Books by Sarah Varland

Love Inspired Suspense

Treasure Point Secrets
Tundra Threat
Cold Case Witness
Silent Night Shadows
Perilous Homecoming
Mountain Refuge
Alaskan Hideout

Visit the Author Profile page at Harlequin.com.

ALASKAN HIDEOUT

SARAH VARLAND

HARLEQUIN® LOVE INSPIRED® SUSPENSE

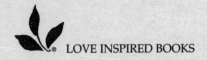

LOVE INSPIRED BOOKS

ISBN-13: 978-1-335-54390-5

Alaskan Hideout

www.Harlequin.com

Printed in U.S.A.

As far as the east is from the west,
so far hath he removed our transgressions from us.
—Psalms 103:12

To Joshua and Timothy, for being the best boys anyone could ask for. You search all my books for a *J* and a *T* to see if those copies are "yours" (oddly enough you've found a *J* or a *T* in every book so far), so here are your names, boys. This one's for you. Thanks for sharing with me your love of stories, for writing them down, telling me stories out loud and letting me read to you. You're both great and I love you. Thanks for letting me work when I need to and for being so excited when this book was finished. And no, you can't read Mommy's books yet, no matter how brave you think you are. But I appreciate it. Love you both!

ONE

Five miles to go. Only five miles.

Emma Bass gripped the steering wheel tighter and checked the rearview mirror one more time, panic rising in her that she might see the car following her—again—even though it had been four thousand miles and over a week since she'd last seen it.

Fifteen days since she'd witnessed the murder of her company's CEO. Fourteen days since she'd started to feel like she was being observed. All the time. Twelve days since her son, Luke, mentioned offhandedly that sometimes he felt like someone was watching him.

Twelve days since she'd realized there was nothing the police there could do to protect her since no one could prove they were in danger. Eleven days since she'd left Dallas. Nobody messed with her kid. She'd done plenty of looking back, but only for her and Luke's safety. Emma knew by now that it was better to let the past be the past and to keep moving forward. At whatever cost. Always. Moving. Forward.

Except now, when she voluntarily blasted herself back eight years to college graduation and her ultimatum to her then boyfriend that she never should have given. Her or his family's lodge.

Emma didn't know why she'd done it. Maybe it had been because the thought of Alaska scared her. She wasn't inept in the country, but there was a difference between the Georgia countryside—lazy, muddy rivers and gently rolling hills—and the rugged Alaskan wilderness Tyler had showed her pictures of. He'd done so eagerly, like he'd thought the picturesque scenery of his beloved Alaska would be enough to convince her to move there with him, get engaged, take some time to get to know the area and his family and then eventually get married.

Instead, every picture of the mountains towering over his ocean-side town had made her shiver a little. There was something so wild about Alaska still. Untamed. Unpredictable.

Emma was a fan of predictable.

Then again, maybe it hadn't been any of

that. Emma might like routine, but she was an adventurer, too, in some ways.

Sighing, she glanced in the rearview mirror and smiled at her seven-year-old's face. Maybe the truth was that she'd taken a pregnancy test the morning of their graduation—and it was positive. And somehow, maybe in a swirl of stress and emotions and being overwhelmed by how her life was changing so quickly, she'd said stupid things to Tyler, things she hadn't been able to take back.

He'd simply walked away. No, that wasn't true. She'd panicked, realized she didn't deserve him and practically *chased* him away. But he hadn't come back. And Emma hadn't been able to handle the idea that he'd marry her only because he felt obligated, didn't want his future decided for him just because someone had decided hers.

So years had passed. She'd said nothing to Tyler. Every single night as she'd lain in bed, trying to fall asleep, desperately trying to convince her mind to stop, she regretted her silence. But every day it became a little harder to break.

Life, ready or not, was about to do it for her.

She'd known when Luke had told her he'd felt like someone was watching him that they were in trouble. Emma had hoped, foolishly, for the first few hours after she'd escaped the crime scene, that maybe she'd be safe. She'd given her report to the police, answered their questions and thought that might actually be the end of it. But if both she and Luke felt like they were being watched, someone was stalking her, most likely the person who'd killed her boss. And the police department's hands were tied. They were good, she respected them. But they weren't a bodyguard service and without solid proof she was in danger, they'd told her all she could do was file a report.

Which wouldn't exactly keep either her or Luke safe.

Emma needed to run and Alaska had seemed like the best option. For one thing, the distance from Dallas made it ideal, especially since it was so far removed from the rest of the United States. Also, Emma figured, a bunch of outdoorsmen carrying guns to protect themselves against bears was about the safest place she could be. Besides—and maybe the most important reason—she'd promised herself if she made it out of the building that night she'd make things right with Tyler. He deserved to know about his son.

Movement behind her caught her attention.

The car that seemed to have been following her had edged closer. Emma tensed. She couldn't see the driver well in the rearview mirror and part of her doubted it was anything to worry about. After all, according to what Tyler had told her, this was the only road to several towns. Traffic tended to clump together and travel together.

Right?

Emma glanced back again, tension tightening her shoulders. She exhaled slowly and stole another glance at her sleeping son. He was okay.

She accelerated a bit, anxious to get to Moose Haven Lodge, an irony that wasn't lost on her as the lodge itself had been part of the reason everything had ended so badly for her and Tyler. He'd talked their entire college career about opening his own inn, maybe on a beach somewhere, starting fresh, and she'd loved the dream almost as much as she'd loved him.

And then out of the blue he'd announced he was returning to Alaska. To his parents' lodge.

Emma couldn't handle the lack of civilization, the dark winters. The cold. The wildlife. The idea that she'd be raising a kid in a place she didn't know, far from everything she understood and all the people she cared about. So she'd told him so. Broken his heart.

It was too late to believe she could restore that relationship. It had been destroyed beyond repair. What she hoped for right now was that she could keep her son safe—and Alaska was the best place she knew of to do that—and, also, maybe that Luke could get to know his dad.

Tyler as a dad.

She shook her head, old feelings churning in her stomach. She'd never stopped loving him, really. There'd just come a point when she'd decided she wasn't going to give up everything she'd ever dreamed of for love.

The car behind her inched closer again and Emma pressed her foot even further on the gas. Was there anywhere she could pull off, like one of those turnouts she'd seen on the highway earlier for slow vehicles? Maybe the car behind her was just in a hurry. It could be as simple and innocuous as that, couldn't it?

She'd just passed the Welcome to Moose Haven sign when everything happened at once. A squeal of tires, the sickening sound of metal on metal, the crunching of her car intermingled with her own screams as the impact pulled her backward and then threw her forward with enough force to smash her head on the steering wheel. Pain exploded behind her left eye and the edges of her vision went dark.

"Mom!" Luke cried, sounding so much younger than seven.

Please, God, keep him safe.

Out of the corner of her eye, Emma saw the car that had hit her speed away in the opposite direction of Moose Haven. Meanwhile her car was still skidding across the road, careering toward the edge of the road and the ravine below.

Emma fumbled for her phone, wishing she could dial 9-1-1, but knowing she didn't have enough time. She hit the brakes, but her tires caught on gravel, sliding off the asphalt too fast for her to correct.

They were going to go over the edge and into the woods below the road.

"Hang on, baby!"

The car tumbled down the side of the road, hitting trees on the way, some of them small enough that the car crushed them. The last one finally was big enough to bring them to a shuddering halt.

Emma felt them stop, heard the reassuring sounds of Luke asking what was going on.

And then everything went black.

* * *

Sirens whirred in the distance and, from the sound of it, they were passing right by the lodge, tearing down the Moose Haven cut-off in the direction of the Seward Highway. As Moose Haven wasn't a big city, sirens weren't an everyday occurrence but accidents happened on the highway often enough that Tyler Dawson wasn't surprised by the sound.

Out of habit, he checked his phone for text messages he might have missed. Due to the lodge's proximity to some of the common accident sites and Tyler's basic EMT certification, his brother, Noah, the police chief of Moose Haven, would sometimes ask for his help. He expected that would be even more true now that he'd graduated from the police academy in Sitka and was technically a Moose Haven Reserve officer. Not a title he'd have ever expected from himself, or one he'd particularly wanted, but when family asked you to do something, you did it. At least Tyler did. And Noah had asked him to do it.

He looked at the phone's screen.

Nothing.

Instead of heading out to help, he said a quick prayer for whoever was involved then went back to the financial statements he'd been going over. He winced at the first bill he looked at, cringed at the second and by the third was ready to close the books and give up on bills for the day.

However he looked at it, Moose Haven Lodge was in trouble. He'd taken over from his parents not quite eight years ago and at first it had gone well. Then the recession that had hit the Lower 48 had finally made its way to Alaska and the lodge had started to feel the strain. Their returning clients weren't able to keep vacationing the way they had been in the past.

Tyler knew what the problem was—they needed more clients—so he'd trimmed expenses where he needed to and the lodge ran well. He was good at his job.

He just wasn't as good at getting the word out and, with the competition bigger lodges brought in, he was struggling.

If you're interested in a struggling mountain lodge, God, I could use some help.

Tyler meant the prayer, meant it with every fiber of his being this morning, amid the bills. However, at the same time, he had to wonder to what degree God was invested in those kinds of details. Had God created him? Yes. Did He care about him? Yes.

But about details like this?

Tyler didn't know. The last time he'd expected God to intervene in the day-to-day details of his life was when he'd prayed he and his college girlfriend could reconcile somehow.

Eight years this spring and they'd never spoken again.

Tyler's phone beeped and he glanced at the message. Noah needed help at the wreck. It was just about two miles from the lodge.

He left a note on the front desk for the tourists he expected to have checking in soon and headed out to his car. In small-town Alaska, communities had to pull together and help each other.

Two miles later Tyler winced at the damage to the small white car—a rental, he guessed from the fact that besides having its back end smashed in, it looked like hordes of others that invaded the Kenai Peninsula area every summer. He prayed again for whoever was inside, then parked his car.

"Female, late twenties, early thirties maybe," Noah said as he approached. "She's in bad shape, but the fire department already has her on the way to the hospital. What I need your help with most is the kid. He needs to be checked out by a doctor, though thankfully he looks okay. But the poor boy's terrified."

"Got it."

Tyler stepped toward the wreckage.

Noah put a hand on his arm, stopping him.

He looked up at his brother, not bothering to hide his annoyance. Did he want his help or not?

"Tyler…the woman…"

"Yes?"

Noah exhaled. "I looked at her license for ID. It's Emma Bass."

Tyler thought he might have stopped breathing. Never mind his own certification, he needed an EMT to look at him right now. Spasms in his chest, palms sweaty. What was she doing in Alaska, near his lodge? She'd broken up with him with little explanation when everything had been going well…too well for their own good at one point…

Kid. Noah had said there was a kid in the car. Now Tyler *knew* he'd stopped breathing.

He was a smart guy. It didn't take long for shock to turn to full-blown panic as other pieces of the puzzle began to fall into place.

He was just about to ask how old the boy was when Noah said, "He says he's seven."

Tyler would guess he'd be eight in—he

did some quick figuring from the worst mistake he'd ever made, the one time he hadn't acted honorably, the way he'd been taught was right—December.

"Wait." Noah gave him a sharp look. "When did you graduate college and break up with Emma?"

"She broke up with me."

"When, Tyler?"

"Eight years ago last spring." He met his brother's eyes, squaring his shoulders, ready for whatever his sibling was going to dish out. He deserved it.

Noah still didn't say anything, so Tyler lowered his voice and muttered, "Yes, okay? Yes, he could be mine." Could be? More like *probably was*, hard as it was to wrap his mind around. He knew Emma wasn't the kind of woman who'd have been unfaithful. This was Tyler's kid, he knew it as certainly as he knew just about anything else in life.

Tyler moved closer to the boy.

"When's your birthday?" He tried to keep his voice light so it would sound like he was just making casual conversation.

"December 17."

Tyler blinked as the kid watched him with

eyes he knew looked remarkably like his own. Green. Mossy green.

This was his kid.

And Emma hadn't told him.

He swallowed hard. "I'm just going to check you out and make sure you're okay and then we'll take you to the hospital to wait on your mom."

The boy nodded, eyes wide. "Okay."

Tyler went through the motions of a typical post-car-crash checkup, doing his best as he heard the words echoing in his mind over and over. *His son. His son. His son.*

"Is my mom going to be okay?"

"They're taking great care of her." Tyler hadn't been able to focus his mind enough to consider whether or not Emma was seriously injured. Surely, Noah would have said…

Still he didn't want to lie to the boy.

But hope won out. "I think she'll be okay." She had to be. Tyler needed to talk to her. The questions he needed to ask her were only growing by the minute.

Only then did he realize he'd never asked the kid his name. He'd been so focused on learning his birthday to confirm what he already knew in his mind.

"What's your name, buddy?"

"I'm Luke Dawson."

Tyler needed to talk to Emma.

Right now.

He took a deep breath and tried to stay calm for the kid, who he'd decided wasn't going to sit in some cold hospital waiting room. So Emma hadn't told him about Luke. A huge deal, one he'd have to sort through in his mind, but he had other things to worry about right now. Like why the damage to the car looked like another vehicle had been involved. The back end of the Toyota was smashed in and some kind of dark paint, black or blue, had left streaks on the side.

"I'll be right back, okay, Luke?"

He stepped away from the car and walked toward his brother. "Where's the other car?"

"Hit and run."

"Is something going to be done about that?"

Noah raised his eyebrows and Tyler checked himself. It wasn't the best idea for him to be telling his brother how to do his job. He held up his hands in surrender. "Sorry. I just want this dealt with." Uneasiness churned in his stomach along with no fewer than ten other emotions he couldn't name at the moment. Emma. A son. Car wreck.

Something about it didn't sit right.

A cell phone rang in the front of the car and both brothers turned to look at it.

Noah gave him a look of warning. "There's no protocol that says you should answer that." He'd read the look on Tyler's face well. Back in his life, not even *in it* technically, for ten minutes, and Emma was already making him do things that weren't like him. She'd loosened him up in college, taught him that having friends was sometimes more important than studying for an exam, and in turn he'd taught her the value of lists, planning, stability.

He moved to the car and answered the call on the unlocked phone before Noah could try to stop him. Because technically there was no protocol that said he shouldn't.

It was an unknown number. His curiosity piqued. "Hello?"

Whoever was on the other end hung up.

"Who was it?" Noah asked.

"No idea."

His questions for Emma, about Emma, were only growing and Tyler's mind was consumed with her presence, even though she wasn't physically there but a few miles away at the Moose Haven Hospital. This was what this woman did to him, made it impossible for him to think, made him feel too much.

What's going on, God? Why is she here? And do You really think I can handle this?

It was that last question Tyler would really like an answer to. Because he wasn't sure he was up to whatever this challenge was. When it came to Emma, with how thoroughly she'd broken his heart, he'd wound up the loser.

TWO

Emma had the worst headache she'd ever had in her life, she was in a strange town and someone appeared to want her dead.

And to top it all off, she was within miles of Tyler Dawson, which meant she was going to have to face him soon…and she still had no idea what she was going to say.

Everything about her current situation terrified her.

Emma sat up in the hospital bed. Luke. Where was Luke? She looked around, frantic. Surely the police who'd come to the scene would recognize that hers hadn't been an ordinary accident, right? And they'd keep her son…*their* son…safe?

She ran back over the details in her mind. The car following too close. The crunch of metal on metal as her car had rolled in the sunlight and then only darkness. She didn't remember anything else.

Emma pressed the call button for the nurse. First order of business, she had to get out of here and go take care of her son. And figure out if the wreck was some kind of weird coincidence or…

A vision of a person with a gun stalking toward her, wanting her dead, solidified in her mind. No, this hadn't been coincidence and there was no point in pretending it could have been. Emma had witnessed a murder, had had the audacity to correct the assumption that it had been suicide, something the bad guys had probably set up on purpose. And now, in their eyes, she had to die.

The only problem was that she had too much to live for. Luke. Her desire to be the best at what she did in her job, even if she was clearly searching for a new one. The drive to convince Tyler to forgive her and maybe, just maybe, let them be friends?

Emma wasn't stupid. She knew he'd never take her back, never forgive the betrayal of keeping their son from him. Every day she'd not told him had driven the nail deeper into the coffin of their relationship and now it was too late.

Too much water under the bridge.

The door of her room creaked open and Emma's shoulders relaxed. If the doctors hadn't planned to discharge her yet, she'd make sure the nurse understood how important it was that she be released.

But it wasn't a nurse. It was Tyler. Looking better than she'd remembered even. Tall, broad-shouldered, with dark hair…and piercing green eyes she'd never been able to intentionally look away from.

Except now. Emma looked down at the hospital bedding. Braced herself.

The room was still. He said nothing. So she looked back up. Swallowed hard.

"Tyler." Emma said his name slowly, hating the injustice in the fact that she was seeing him again for the first time in almost a decade wearing a blue hospital gown, with at least one cut on her face, hair matted with blood.

Not the impression she'd have preferred to make, but then again, there were lots of things about her life that weren't how she would have preferred them. "I know you must hate me," she continued, "But is Luke okay?"

He gave the slightest of nods and then speared her with his gaze.

"How. Could. You."

Emma looked into his eyes, realizing now that she'd always done that when she'd wanted to know what he was thinking. She had always thought she could see more in people's gazes than others could, like she could see inside them. Someone had told her that before…

Oh, Tyler.

Her cheeks heated, embarrassment, regret and a maelstrom of other emotions all swirling inside her.

"I'm sorry." It seemed a good place to start.

"I appreciate that." His voice was measured and even. This was the Tyler she'd met at the start of college, the Tyler who'd not make a step without considering the implications to his five-year plan, the one who'd known where he was headed and had been so solid in his convictions.

Except that one night…

"I am, Tyler. For…for all of it." She swallowed hard, still feeling responsible for the time their innocent relationship had derailed. "Not for Luke's existence, though. I won't be sorry for that." She heard her tone harden as she remembered what she'd given up for him. Her parents hadn't spoken to her since right after she'd given birth when they'd tried to convince her that just because she'd "insisted" on having Luke, didn't mean she had to keep him. They'd brought up adoption and while she'd thought adoption was a wonderful thing, it hadn't been what she'd wanted.

At all.

"Obviously."

Emma exhaled. At least Tyler seemed to understand that Luke's life was a gift. She watched emotions chase across his face and sat there facing him, not knowing what to do. What to say.

"Why are you here? And why is someone trying to kill you?"

Emma let out of a breath.

The door swung open again, both their attentions going that way.

A man in uniform walked in.

"This is my brother, Police Chief Noah Dawson. He'll do what he can to help you, but you'll have to give him some answers."

Emma nodded.

"And I'd like some of those, too."

Again her cheeks burned. "I'll give them to you, the ones I have." She pressed the nurse call button. "I'm assuming they were planning to discharge me soon. I'll tell them it needs to be now."

Noah looked between them, shook his head.

"Let's get out of the hospital to somewhere we can talk comfortably. I've got my car out front. Emma, Tyler, why don't the two of you climb in and we'll drive to the station? Do you have...regular clothes, Emma?"

She shook her head. "I'm not sure. I think they might have been stained from the wreck." Her hand went to the spot on her forehead. The wound wasn't too large but head wounds bled a lot.

"I'll have my sister Kate bring you something. She's about your size."

Emma nodded, thankful. Even if the clothes swallowed her, as garments often did—she was only five-two—anything was better than a hospital gown.

The nurse walked in just then, with the good news that the doctor had agreed to her discharge. When her papers were done, Emma tied a second hospital gown around the back of herself so she could at least walk without being exposed in any way even if she did look ridiculous.

She glanced in Tyler's direction as they walked toward the car, careful to stay sandwiched between the two men yet feeling the tension radiating off both of them. She'd been lying to herself. She'd told herself Tyler would never forgive her, but somewhere deep inside, hope had flickered.

Its flames were completely extinguished now.

He'd never forgive her.

Tyler's jaw was clamped so tight he was getting a headache. He glanced at his watch. Just past four in the afternoon and he felt like he'd lived three lifetimes since he'd gotten called out to help with the wreck just after lunch.

Emma Bass was in town.

She had a son.

He had a son.

She hadn't told him.

His mind kept spinning in circles over those indisputable facts, with enough questions mixed in to make him feel physically ill. It was like he'd run too many miles without stopping for food or water and was full-body exhausted. But in his mind the biggest question was what he had done so wrong.

Besides the obvious. He'd handled their relationship well the entire time they were in college, balanced his emotions with his faith, his convictions. His sense of right and wrong. The one time he hadn't…

Noah had grilled him on the drive to the

hospital, more stunned than Tyler about him having a son, if such a thing was possible. Noah was the oldest, Tyler next, but somehow Tyler had always felt like his siblings looked up to him. He was the stable one, the one to always be counted on. He had to be defined by something, do something noteworthy even if it was just being the dependable sibling, with Noah saving the world from crime, Kate making a name for herself as one of the best trackers in Alaska, and Summer running on mountains, at the top of the world without flinching.

Tyler? Tyler was just dependable. It was what he was good at.

Until now.

He felt the weight of Noah's disappointment, had wanted to defend himself, but knew there was no use. Summer's reaction was the one he was bracing himself for. Tyler had known she'd beat herself up over her own past but he hadn't shared a word of his. Hopefully his little sister would understand it just hadn't been the right time to share his story.

Emma Bass was in town.

His mind looped back as he looked over at the woman next to him in the back of the police cruiser. The cut on her forehead, her pale skin, the hospital attire… All of it reminded him that no matter what questions he had about their past, someone was after Emma and, for some reason, she'd felt it best to come to Alaska. Knowing she was in danger made it difficult for him to breathe, the physical impact unexpected but intense enough that Tyler knew he needed to find a way to compartmentalize his feelings until she was ready to talk, to separate himself emotionally so he could help Noah in whatever capacity he was needed.

He knew the Moose Haven PD was small-town, though the department now had its biggest complement in years with four officers now that Clay had joined the force. Still, they didn't have an excess of manpower and Tyler couldn't see Noah putting someone on Emma full-time since they hadn't been able to do that when a serial killer was after his sister few months ago.

An idea settled in his mind. Tyler wasn't an officer, but he'd been to the police academy in Sitka, had just finished the training recently. Noah had wanted more reserve officers just in case. Even though he didn't have a lot of experience, Tyler could technically do the job.

If it came down to it, Tyler would do what he had to do to keep Emma safe.

Not because he still felt anything for her. But because it was the right thing to do.

Noah turned left when he should have turned right.

"I thought you were taking us to the station?" Tyler asked from behind the Plexiglas.

Noah shook his head. "I changed my mind. Emma needs to be somewhere comfortable, right?" He looked back at her and Tyler saw a small smile on Emma's face at the consideration. "She'd probably like to see for herself that her son is okay, too."

"He's at the lodge, not at the police station?"

Was that alarm in her voice? Tyler had talked about his family all the time in college and even if Emma had never had the chance to meet them, she should know that they were good people. Dependable.

Of course, she should have known the same thing about him.

Noah spoke up. "He's safe there with my sisters. They're two of the toughest people I know and I left them there with Clay Hitchcock, one of my best officers."

Emma's face relaxed a little. "I know Clay. From college."

"That's right, I'd forgotten that," Noah said. No one responded and the rest of the drive passed in silence as they drove out of town, away from the bay and into the deep woods of the northern edge of town.

A short time later the cruiser pulled up in front of Moose Haven Lodge and Tyler glanced up at it, trying to see his family lodge through Emma's eyes.

Their relationship, already on rocky soil after their life-altering mistake, had fallen apart when he'd scrapped his plans to open his own lodge on a beach somewhere and had agreed to take over this one for his parents so they could retire. She'd refused to leave Texas for *Alaska*, said the name of his home state like it was the literal end of the earth, unsettled and uninhabitable. He hoped the gorgeous log-sided lodge in front of her made her feel... something.

Regret? Tyler didn't know...that wasn't right to wish on anyone. But he did somehow hope she saw how wrong she'd been about his ability to provide a nice life for them.

Apparently for the baby they'd had on the way.

Noah parked the car and Emma got out. Tyler followed.

"Wow." She turned to him as she took the first couple steps to the wide front porch. "This is nothing like I pictured."

"I didn't figure it would be."

She met his eyes and, for half a second, it was as if the last eight years hadn't happened, as though nothing had even gone wrong. He stood still for a minute—not caring that his brother was watching—temporarily pushing away the hurt in Emma's rejection, the anger that she'd kept the fact that he was a dad from him.

And then it all came rushing back all at once. He turned away. But not before he saw her smile fade as she jumped and flinched almost as though he'd hit her, something he'd never do, had never even thought of doing.

He didn't like how much Emma made him *feel*. She'd always done that, magnified his life, made it more vivid, brighter, fuller.

Right up until she'd left.

Tyler walked past her, up to the lodge. He looked back only long enough to confirm that Noah was with her. "Will she be okay with you for a minute?" He lowered his voice unconsciously as he swallowed back everything he felt.

Noah nodded.

Tyler hurried inside. He just needed a few minutes.

A dad. He was a dad.

With a woman he'd loved like he'd never loved anyone else. A woman he could never have.

THREE

"Luke!"

She'd no sooner stepped into the lobby of Moose Haven Lodge when her son came flying into her arms. Gathering him close, Emma squeezed him hard and thanked God for keeping him safe when she'd been forced off the road and into the ravine. She suspected that was one of the things Noah was going to want to talk about, and Emma was ready to tell him the story, though she could use a few minutes to decompress.

Things between her and Tyler had never been easy. Even as best friends before they'd officially started dating there'd been a sizzling current of electricity between them. It made sense that their breakup would be more like a devastating explosion of fireworks. Even this long afterward.

She kept her arms around Luke, thankful

that at least Tyler hadn't said anything negative about her son, thankful he'd been safe.

"Emma, if you want to come with me, I'll get you some clothes."

A woman Emma hadn't seen before was standing nearby, along with another woman and a man. The woman who'd spoken to her was small, dark haired, and with a look on her face like nothing got past her. She had to be Kate. The taller woman, the one with the blond hair and soft waves, she recognized as Tyler's sister, Summer, who was a mountain runner. Emma'd never have known the sport existed if it wasn't for Tyler, but she'd followed it a bit online over the years, desperate enough for a glimpse into Tyler's world. Keeping up to date with his sister had helped her to fill that void in some small way. Summer had been out of competition for years—Emma suspected there was a story there—but lately rumors were flying that she might be getting back into it. The man next to her was with the Moose Haven PD and she recognized him from college. Clay Hitchcock.

"Yes, please, I'd love to change."

Kate motioned for her to follow her up the stairs and Emma did so, relieved to be away from Tyler. Had she remembered how tall he was, the broadness of his shoulders?

Memory flashed in her mind. Yes. She'd remembered, somewhere inside. She'd just chosen to forget.

It had been better for both of them that way.

"Is Luke okay with Summer and Clay, do you think?"

"More than okay," Kate assured her as she led her into a room at the top of the stairs. "Summer and Clay are basically the unbeatable team. You should hear sometime what happened to Summer a few months ago. Although I guess it's not the kind of story you want to hear when someone is after you. Sorry." She offered an apologetic smile.

Emma smiled back.

These were the people she'd accused Tyler of valuing more than her? First of all, the accusation had been empty, borne of some desire to hurt him and a desperation to see if he'd choose her, if he'd cared enough to make things permanent. Tyler had always held his emotions in check and while she'd known in college that he'd loved her, it had been hard to tell how much.

Maybe she'd panicked when she'd seen the two lines on the pregnancy test stick. She hadn't had a doubt that once he'd found out, Tyler would marry her immediately...

But Emma hadn't wanted that, hadn't wanted to be chosen only because it was the "right" thing to do or because of the baby she'd carried. She'd spent her life in her parent's high-society circles, being chosen because she was popular, known the right people, could network the right way.

For once, she'd wanted to be chosen because she was Emma. Just for her.

Tyler had loved her for her. She'd thought so, at least. And yet it hadn't been enough. Not that it mattered now. Nothing did except keeping Luke and herself safe.

Kate handed Emma the spare clothes and she smiled gratefully. "Thanks, I can't wait to be out of these."

"Kinda rough seeing your ex for the first time in a hospital gown, huh?" Kate's half grin softened the words. Emma guessed the woman was probably just a straight shooter who didn't sugar coat much. She seemed to remember Tyler telling her that Alaskans were often like that.

"Beyond rough. At least it wasn't the worst part of today."

"I guess not. You're in good hands, though. Our family protects its own."

"I'm not…"

Kate just stared at her. "Isn't Luke Tyler's son?"

Emma nodded.

"Then even if Tyler never speaks to you again, that makes me Luke's aunt. And that makes you family. In a weird way, maybe, but we're not going to let anything happen to you, Emma."

Tears stung the corners of her eyes. When was the last time someone had stood up for her like that? Welcomed her so unquestioningly? Emma didn't know.

"I'll be right outside the door. You so much as squeak and I'm coming back in, okay?" Kate stepped out.

Emma took the clothes and changed, grateful to have something to wear and also making a mental note to ask Noah what had happened to her car so she could retrieve their belongings. Though, for now, she was incredibly grateful to Kate for the black hiking pants and green Moose Haven Lodge sweatshirt. Emma stole a glance at herself in the mirror before letting Kate back inside and winced. The sweatshirt set off her blue eyes nicely, and her hair wasn't so bad, but nothing could mask the cut on her forehead.

Not that it mattered. There was no one here she needed to try to impress...was there?

She opened the door and Kate smiled. "You look nice. They're waiting for you downstairs. Noah really wants to know what you're mixed up in that has someone after you."

"Ever heard of being in the wrong place at the wrong time?" Emma asked as she headed down the stairs.

She found Noah and Tyler both sitting in the family room. No sign of the others she'd seen on her way in, Luke included. "Where's my son?"

Was it her imagination or did Tyler flinch at the "my" part of that? Fine, *their* son, but it didn't seem natural to say that when she'd said it the other way for so long.

"Clay and Summer took him upstairs to the TV room to watch *Finding Nemo*."

Emma's shoulders relaxed a little as she nodded. She looked at the two men, sitting in chairs, and took a spot on the sofa. "Where do you want me to start?"

"With whatever happened that made this guy come after you."

"That started after work one night when I

went back to confront my boss about some in-consistencies in paperwork I'd stumbled upon. I assume it has something to do with that."

"You did financial stuff?" Noah asked.

She shook her head. "Marketing. It was truly an accident I ever saw it, but once I had, I couldn't ignore it. It looked too much like money laundering or something."

"Did you ask your boss about it?"

She shook her head. "That's when I saw him get shot."

Noah's eyes widened. "You witnessed it?"

Emma stole a glance at Tyler. His face was steady, solid, unreadable. Just like it had been when she'd met him. They'd both changed over the years they'd been together, but she guessed time had changed them even more.

"Murderers don't often like to leave wit-nesses alive."

Emma laughed nervously, desperate to cover her vulnerability. "I'd rather change that this time. I'm all Luke has. I mean, I *was* all he had until now but… I'm his mom. And he still needs me."

Noah nodded. "We're not going to let them get to you, Emma. You made the right choice coming here. We've got your back."

There he was, making her tear up again like

Kate had. What was it with this family and their mile-wide protective streak? Not that she was complaining.

She wasn't alone anymore. Not completely.

Emma glanced Tyler's direction again. How did he feel about all this? She wished she knew, but didn't expect him to divulge what he was feeling. He just wasn't like that.

"Tell me more about that night," Noah said. "And everything after it."

Emma did so, including the fact that the newspapers had initially reported it as a suicide, how she'd called Officer Smith, how Mike had been killed. And how she'd come here.

Noah listened carefully, nodding in the right spots. "I'm going to need to think about this. For today you'll stay here." He looked at Kate. "Maybe you guys could go join them watching that movie?"

Kate stood and motioned for Emma to follow. She did, but slower, her legs finally feeling the weight of the day.

Noah's and Tyler's voices carried up the stairs as they talked.

Too curious not to, Emma paused.

"…constant protection…" Noah's voice.

"…spare enough officers…" Tyler.

"No... But you..."

"Are you serious, Noah? *Me* protect her?"

Emma swallowed hard, hurrying the rest of the way up the stairs without looking back. It was bad enough she needed protection. And while she still felt she'd done the right thing in coming here, it hurt to hear those words from Tyler. She'd wondered how he felt about all this. Well, now she knew.

He wanted nothing to do with her.

Night fell faster this time of year and it took Tyler off guard tonight more than it usually did. The spruce trees had darkened to their fall color, which had always seemed to him to be a darker green than the one they had in the summer, and everything around the lodge was blackness, or close to it.

Tonight he felt the blackness inside him, fear wrapping around his heart and gripping tight. Emma wasn't his anymore, never had been officially. He'd planned to ask her to marry him on graduation day, had assumed they'd get married that summer in Alaska, along the edge of Half Mile Lake, the mountain lake he'd hike to on breaks from college. Back then he hadn't planned to live there. He'd wanted a change, but he'd known the vividness of Emma's personality would appreciate the extremes of Alaska, even if it wasn't the city lifestyle she was used to.

He took a deep breath, walked down the hall to the room where she was staying and lifted a hand to knock on the door.

She took so long to answer that he considered bursting inside until he remembered Kate was in there. No one was getting past his sister. She was easily the toughest person he knew, him and Noah included. He laughed a little at the thought of petite Kate and how tough she was. The man who won her heart one day would have to be some kind of special.

Of course, what did Tyler know about romance? Not much, obviously.

The door cracked open slightly.

Emma stepped out, her blue eyes as deep and easy to stare at as they'd ever been, her hair down around her shoulders in medium brown waves. Soft. He swallowed hard as he reminded himself that reaching out to touch it would be so many levels of inappropriate. Not to mention undesirable. She'd broken his heart once, shattered it, in fact. Chances were good he'd never recover, never find anyone he felt as strongly about as Emma, but maybe that was for the best. She was living, walking proof of the fact that he couldn't trust his feelings, couldn't trust his heart to anyone. And she wasn't asking him to now. All she was asking was for him to help keep her, and their son, safe.

Surely he could do that.

No emotions involved. At least where Emma was concerned. Tyler's eyes moved to the boy who looked so much like both of them and he swallowed hard. He had plenty of feelings where Luke was concerned. Not that he was sure what all of them were yet, but one was a pretty strong fatherly love. No matter what had happened between himself and Emma, the hundreds of ways their imploded relationship had affected their lives, he was glad Luke existed. Couldn't wait to get to know him. After he'd ensured Luke and his mom were both safe.

"What do you want?" she whispered, drawing his attention back to her more than Tyler would have preferred. Just the sound of her voice still gave him shivers, starting in his shoulders, down his chest to his toes.

Yeah, maybe talking to her alone was a bad idea, after all. All Tyler had wanted was some answers, ones that weren't pertinent to the case, that he hadn't gotten earlier.

"Never mind. Sorry. Stay safe, okay?" He turned, was halfway down the hallway when he heard her door shut. He exhaled.

And jumped at the feeling of a hand on his shoulder.

He whirled and Emma jumped back, eyes wide.

"I'm sorry. You scared me."

"You thought I'd just go back to my room, ignore whatever you came here to ask me?" Her eyebrows raised.

"Why do you think I wanted to ask you anything?"

She stared at him. "I know you, Tyler. I used to, anyway, better than anyone maybe." Emma cleared her throat, expression and confidence wavering. "Maybe I don't anymore but… I expected you'd have questions."

"I do."

She nodded. "Want to go downstairs?"

Was it too open down there? The windows behind the great room of the lodge and the family's private living room looked out on the dark woods. If they sat down there with any lights on, anyone watching would be able to see straight into the room, which struck him as a bad idea. Bedrooms weren't appropriate.

The balcony off the hallway? It faced the

parking lot, where at least one policeman, Officer Rogers, was watching. Maybe that was their best—safest—option.

"Follow me." He led her down the hallway, staying on alert as he knew that nowhere was one hundred percent safe. He'd listened to what she'd told Noah that afternoon and felt his heart sinking the more she spoke. She'd had to go and witness a murder. And murderers didn't tend to like witnesses. At least not ones left alive.

Tyler opened the balcony door, stepped out and shut off the hall light behind them.

"What are you doing?" Emma's whisper was accusatory, untrusting.

Tyler flinched.

"I'm making sure we aren't backlit. No one needs to be able to see us out here."

"You think someone is watching?"

"I don't know, Emma." Her name fell off his lips so easily, like he hadn't gone eight years without saying it, no matter how many times he'd thought about her. "We can't be too safe."

She followed him out and they each took an Adirondack chair. When it was light outside, this spot had a view of the parking lot and, beyond that, of Hope Mountain and Sunrise Ridge. Halfway up Sunrise Ridge there was the tarn he'd imagined taking Emma to. Emerald Lake, which almost glowed, the color was such a pure, brilliant blue-green.

It hurt to sit here with her, so close physically but far away in every other way that mattered. Tyler wrestled in his mind. What did he do? Noah had assumed that Tyler would be involved in protecting Emma, that he'd want to be. Tyler appreciated the vote of confidence from his law-enforcement brother, the acknowledgment that he was capable. But maybe he should step away, let someone else take this on. How was he supposed to spend so much time with her?

Then again, there was Luke to consider. Did he want his son to grow up thinking he was a coward who ran from trouble, who'd left his mom to fend for herself?

No, he didn't want that. He had to think of Luke, had to think like a dad. Something that still made his head spin.

"Where do you want to start?"

Emma's voice was soft, not defensive. He didn't know how to respond to her softness. If she'd been angry, upset the way she had been the last few times they'd spoken...

"You knew about the baby. Didn't you?" It hadn't been one of his planned questions, but it had popped out just now as he'd thought about the way she'd talked to him at graduation, the way she'd reacted.

Her shoulders fell. "Yes. I found out that morning."

He replayed everything he remembered about the day, which was most of the details. The way his tie had been too tight. The way he'd stood a little taller, proud of his academic accomplishments and ready to close this chapter so he and Emma could move on.

The angry, accusatory words she'd said to him. Her assertion that she was never moving to Alaska. That his family was more important to him than she was—a statement that had seemed unfounded to him but had hurt nonetheless. That they'd had a nice few years but, you know, maybe they should both move on.

Move on. As though they'd had some kind of casual, passing relationship.

"But you didn't tell me."

"No."

"You should have."

"Yes."

Their words were quiet in the night, barely breaking the silence. Tyler kept his tone low, determined to keep his emotions under control and needing all the help he could get with that.

He also hesitated to alert anyone that *could* be watching nearby that they were relatively exposed. He didn't know if that was why Emma kept her voice whisper-soft or not.

"I'm a dad, Emma. And I didn't know."

She didn't say anything. He looked in her direction, wanting to know how she was feeling. As he shifted his gaze, something caught his eye in the darkness beyond the parking lot. Officer Rogers patrolling?

Or someone stalking them in the darkness? Stalking Emma?

"Tyler…"

"Shh." He held his hand up in front of him. She blinked at him, kept going.

"No, you have to let me."

"I see something. Someone."

She went silent. Still.

His heart thudded in his chest. His hand moved toward the gun he'd left in his waistband holster, concealed by the fleece vest he'd worn today for warmth.

"What is it? Should I go inside?"

She cared what he thought, wanted to know his opinion.

Tyler scanned the darkness in front of them. The wrong choice could be deadly. Move quickly inside and they'd have cover. Even if it had seemed safe, he never should have brought her out here without the benefit of walls to stop or to at least slow a bullet.

Stay still and they might escape notice, might see the person coming after her.

Tyler didn't know which option to choose. So he chose the second. Kept them still, didn't flinch.

The shadow stopped moving. Maybe he'd been imagining it, was jumpy from the adrenaline rush of this entire thing.

And then the shooting started, the first two shots coming in close succession, cracking in the night, shattering the quiet and the windows. Wood flew off the balcony railing in front of them.

Emma screamed.

"Get inside!" Tyler yelled and reached for the door, pulling Emma out of the chair with the other hand.

More shots.

Emma dove as glass shattered.

And she let out another cry.

FOUR

Emma couldn't breathe, the sounds around her, the noise, the flash of glass as it passed her, creating a cacophony of senses that made it impossible to find her balance. Her center.

Sharp pain registered in her cheek and arm. Shards from the window. She couldn't imagine how hard they were going to be to get out.

Tyler, beside her, was immediately on his feet, reached for the weapon on his hip, some kind of medium-size handgun, black. Tyler had a gun? Steady, calm Tyler?

Besides, hadn't she just overheard him telling Noah he wasn't going to help protect her?

Emma had too many questions and not enough time to think them through. Right now she needed to get somewhere safe. Forcing herself to focus, she pushed into the hallway, edged as far away from the door that led to the balcony as she could. Away from danger.

Tyler ran toward it, pushing back out into the darkness. More shots.

"Tyler!"

She swallowed hard, watched as he took cover behind the railing as best he could.

Footsteps behind her. Someone yelling Tyler's name. Noah, also with a gun in his hands.

Emma scooted farther inside, the carpet rough against her hands.

"Get inside!" Noah ordered his brother.

Tyler hesitated, eyes trained on something out there in the night that Emma couldn't see. Didn't want to see. He lowered his gun and followed Noah into the hallway.

The shots stopped.

But nothing felt the same to Emma. Nothing felt safe. If she'd thought her sense of security had been rocked before, this was a whole new level. Someone had gone to the trouble to come after her *again*. Here at a crowded lodge with witnesses everywhere.

Was the killer brave? Cocky? Crazy?

Her trail of thoughts surprised her. She'd have thought she'd be content to leave the investigation in the hands of police, where it belonged, but all of a sudden she didn't want to be in the dark anymore. What if she knew something, more than just the vague recollection of having suspicious papers she'd wanted to talk to her boss about?

What if she could help take down the guy who was after her? Bring security back to her life? Back to the life of this family she'd intruded into? This family whose world she felt she was wrecking as thoroughly as was possible.

They were not only dealing with the danger she'd brought to their doorstep, but they were absorbing what had to be shock at the revelation that her son was part of their family. They all seemed ecstatic, or at least welcoming. And Emma knew her son was the best thing in her life besides Jesus. But for these people to have welcomed her with so much grace despite the fact that her presence, *Luke*'s presence, told them things about their brother that rocked their perception of him…

It hurt to think that she was bringing danger to the first people from whom she'd felt such acceptance in years…or ever. What an odd place to find it, too.

"Get Emma into one of the rooms. I'm going outside to check it out." Noah moved away.

"Let me come, too." Tyler's words were firm. Like he wasn't going to take no for an answer and Emma's heart thudded in her chest.

"I thought you wanted out of this?"

"I'm not going to let anything happen to her. I've got that police academy training you had me get."

Noah nodded. "Fine. Come with me. Kate, keep her safe."

Emma hadn't noticed Kate, but there she was, behind them. She held a hand out to Emma, a look of compassion on her face. "Come on. Luke heard the noise and woke up, but I've got him in my room with Summer. We'll go in there."

Emma nodded. Had Luke heard the shots or just the noises? For his sake she hoped just the noise. She didn't believe in lying to her son, even to protect him, but it didn't seem age-appropriate to explain the full depth of the fact that someone wanted her dead. She'd stuck to vague explanations like "dangerous" and "not safe" on her way here. Things like that. Not "a bad guy is hunting Mommy with his gun."

His. Emma had assumed it was a man but, actually, based on the frame of the figure dressed in black at her office, the one who'd killed her boss, it could have been a woman. Whoever it was had been significantly taller than Emma. Maybe five-nine? Five-ten?

"He's really okay?" she asked Kate on their

way down the hall as she tried to calm her racing heartbeat. Everything had gone from chaos to controlled, thoughtful in such a span of a few seconds. She was having trouble keeping up.

"He's fine, Emma. We're going to make sure he stays that way. You, too."

Emma shook her head as they approached the door to Kate's room and took a deep breath to try to ease some of the tension from her facial features for Luke's sake. "Tyler wants nothing to do with me. He hates me, Kate, and I don't blame him."

Kate shook her head. "The first thing may be true. But he's out there in the dark trying to catch whoever is after you. That doesn't sound like someone who hates you."

They moved into the room and Emma threw her arms open for Luke who immediately jumped off the bed he was on and ran to her, throwing his arms around her and squeezing as tight as he could. It wasn't the most comfortable embrace, but Emma loved her little guy and he was one hundred percent boy. He did nothing halfway. She squeezed back.

"I heard a noise and I was worried about you." He frowned at her. "It's because of the reason why it's dangerous for us to stay in

Texas, right? Because of why we had to come to Alaska?"

Emma met his eyes, wrestled with how to answer, and finally kissed his nose.

"I love you, buddy."

"You didn't answer my question."

"I didn't. You're a smart kid, you know that? Yes, there was something…dangerous. But it's okay. It'll be okay."

Luke seemed satisfied with that and ran back to the bed where Emma now noticed Summer was holding an iPad. She met the other woman's eyes and Summer shrugged. "Sorry, I know I'm totally encouraging the screen time today but…"

Emma smiled. "No explanation needed. A day of movie watching never hurt anyone. Extenuating circumstances and all that." She moved toward them, settled on the other side of Luke, between him and the window. Kate seemed to notice and moved to put herself between Emma and the window. Just like that, she'd make sure Emma and her son were protected? Her chest constricted. She didn't know if she'd ever known this kind of loyalty that didn't ask for anything in return.

Except… Tyler.

She swallowed hard as she thought of him now, out there in the darkness, risking his life.

For her? Because it was the right thing to do?

For Luke?

Emma didn't know and it didn't matter. Any explanation squeezed her heart in a way she couldn't explain and didn't want to analyze too closely because the facts were this: Emma had told herself a lot of half truths over the years to protect her heart, to move forward with her life. She'd had good intentions, truly she had, but everything was clear now that she was here again, with Tyler.

He might have been out of her life for years, but her heart betrayed her. They could never be together, could never get past the entire ocean of water under the bridge that was their relationship, but she was never going to be able to shove him out of the space he occupied in her heart.

It would never come to anything…

But she knew now, as of tonight, that she was never going to stop loving him.

Tyler and Noah spent the next hour canvassing the grounds of the lodge, looking for any sign of their perpetrator, but so far they'd come up with nothing, not the man himself, nor any evidence of where he'd been.

"He had to have left a trail and if we can find where he was shooting from, we might find evidence," Noah had explained to Tyler, though he'd known as much. Earlier this year he'd gone through the entire police academy class in Sitka. Noah had been asking him to for years, and when he'd seen how difficult it had been for the Moose Haven Police Department to work a major case firsthand, as shorthanded as they were this summer when it had involved his sister Summer, he'd finally decided to go through with it. He'd just returned a couple of weeks ago. The class couldn't have been more timely, apparently.

"We need Kate." Tyler finally said what he guessed they both were thinking. They were both trained, tracking had been part of the curriculum at the academy, but Kate had a gift like no one he'd ever seen and could read the signs in the woods better than most people could read a book.

Noah nodded. "You go inside, stay with Summer, Emma and Luke."

Tyler swallowed hard. He hadn't had much time with the boy yet. Everything had been so crazy. Or was that an excuse? Was it really because he was still having trouble adjusting to the fact that he was a *dad*?

He walked into the lodge, a place more familiar to him than any on earth, taking the stairs to his family's bedrooms with heavy steps. They were up there, waiting for him. Blowing out a breath, he raked a hand through his hair. What was Emma expecting from him? After everything that had happened between the two of them, he'd dedicated his life to playing by the rules. He'd been a good son, a good brother, had come home after his parents had announced their retirement to South Carolina, had remained after they'd died. He'd given up his plans for the future to do the right thing.

How on earth was he supposed to proceed now?

Questions unanswered, he turned the knob and pushed open the heavy wooden door, thankful that the lodge was so well built and solid. He didn't know that it technically provided any more security if someone was desperate to get to Emma, but he appreciated the feeling that it did anyway.

She met his eyes as soon as he walked in. He swallowed hard, unable to deny that something flickered in his chest when she looked at him. She'd been the only girl—woman, really—he'd ever loved. The only one to break his heart. He'd tried to date a few women from Moose Haven since he'd been back, mostly to keep his family quiet about his personal life or lack thereof, but nothing had lasted more than a date. None of them was Emma.

He offered her a small smile and she looked away.

He hated this. Hated the fact that there were no women like her but that she wasn't who he'd thought she was, either.

The woman he was in love with was college-aged Emma, a figment from the past. A woman who'd been confident, sure of herself, with just enough vulnerability to make it difficult to get close to her but not so much that it had been impossible. She'd been Tyler's opposite in many ways. He'd always been on the serious side, quick to honor his commitments and to fulfill his duties and Emma was…joy and laughter. She'd had good character, too, had followed through with things she'd committed to. It wasn't that she was careless. She was just somehow lighter than he was.

But maybe people like Emma could do that. The biggest rule Tyler had ever broken had ended up with both their hearts shattered, their relationship ended forever and a little boy who didn't know his dad.

Tyler swallowed hard. He could really use some time outside, maybe at the archery range. There was just something cathartic about the feeling of a bow in his hands, his hand tight around the grip, the tautness of the bowstring in his fingers as he drew it back. You couldn't shoot a bow angry. Not well. You had to calm your breathing, slow down. Focus.

He'd spent hours with that bow in the weeks after college graduation.

"Everything okay?" Summer asked him.

Tyler had no idea how to answer but decided to go with the easiest reference to what was going on right now with the shooting situation. "Seems to be. As okay as it can be." He shrugged. "We couldn't find anything. That's why we sent Kate out."

"Kate?" Emma's eyebrows raised.

"She's the best tracker I've ever met." Tyler moved farther into the room, eyed the iPad. "What are you watching, buddy?" he asked Luke, deciding maybe talking to the boy directly was the best move at this point. He couldn't seem to do anything right where Luke's mom was concerned, no matter how much some part of him wished he was able to.

"The Incredibles." He looked up from the screen, at Tyler. There was something so surreal about gazing into eyes that looked just like his own.

"That's a good one. It's a family of superheroes, right?" He and Emma had seen it together.

"Yep. They've all got special powers. I can run fast like that, almost as fast." And just that quick he was up off the bed, iPad forgotten. "Want to see?"

"It's nighttime, Luke." Emma's voice was tired. He looked at her quickly, then glanced away before she noticed.

"Maybe another time."

"Because of the danger?"

This time Tyler swung his gaze to Emma intentionally and waited to see what she would say. Had she told Luke about everything that was happening?

"Yes, baby."

"I'm not a baby," Luke protested, but climbed back onto the bed, over Emma and snuggled in next to her.

Wow. The way he loved her, trusted her.

Tyler hadn't spent much time around kids. There were some at his church, but he figured they were sort of the responsibility of their parents and maybe the single women who seemed to love holding babies. And, of course, families stayed at the lodge. But he was so busy with the job now, working to make the lodge more profitable, that he often didn't have time to stop and watch people the way he had when he'd worked here during the summers for his parents.

Moose Haven Lodge in its heyday, when his parents were here, had never had money troubles. At least, not that Tyler knew of. His parents had the kinds of magnetic personalities that made guests return time and again. People had felt welcomed in a way that Tyler hadn't been able to replicate, no matter how many things he felt like he was doing right.

A small problem in the midst of Emma's life being in danger, but it was in the back of his mind anyway.

He wanted to talk to her, to ask her to come with him out of this room, away from the curious eyes of his sister. He didn't blame Summer for having questions, too. He'd been wrong to not share his own past, his own pain with his sister.

He should apologize to her. But not now, it wasn't the time. Right now he needed to finish that conversation with Emma. He had to clear the air. It hurt the way she hadn't told him, the way she looked away from him, trusted every single member of his family more than she did him. Tyler hadn't done anything to deserve that. Not that he could think of. He'd loved her at one time. Had always tried to show it.

And she'd left. With his unborn son a secret.

The door eased open. Tyler tensed, hand on his weapon, which was still holstered. It was Kate.

"Noah wants you outside, Tyler."

"You found it?"

She raised her eyebrows. "Did you doubt that I would?"

"Of course not." Tyler took a last look at Emma. At Luke.

And then he walked out the door, shutting it behind him.

FIVE

Emma couldn't decide if she could breathe easier when Tyler left or when he was in the room with her. When he was gone she felt... not as safe. Like she was missing something. And when he was there she held her breath, waiting for the fallout that still hadn't quite come down from the choices she'd made years ago. The bad ones. Like leaving town without telling him about the results of the pregnancy test. And the way she'd taken a photo of Luke at Christmas every year since then, intending to send them to Tyler with an explanation, and yet never had.

She glanced over at her son to find that in the last few moments he'd managed to nod off. Good. Maybe she could get some answers about the threat they were dealing with without scaring Luke.

"So what did Noah say? Anything?" Emma

asked Kate, not just because she was curious but to take her mind out of the dark place it was headed. Regrets never did any good. Isn't that was her father had always said?

Another subject she wanted to avoid. She focused her attention on Tyler's sister, awaiting her answer.

"We found the spot where the shooter was. It's good, not too impressive a range, just basically far enough into the darkness to avoid being seen."

"So, not a professional?" Emma knew she was guessing, acting like her crime scene TV show knowledge was useful in this situation, but it was all she had and she didn't want to be left out.

Kate looked impressed at her guess, anyway. "That would be my thought, but I'm not law enforcement."

"What do you do, Kate?"

"I work here at the lodge doing whatever Tyler needs."

"And she's volunteer Search and Rescue. That's what she does with a lot of her time," Summer broke in.

Kate shrugged. "Yeah, that, too."

"Wow, that's a lot! Did you always want to work at the lodge?" Emma was curious, despite any warnings in her head that she didn't belong here, should hold Tyler's family at arm's length so they wouldn't hurt her, either. They might like her well enough now, as Luke's mom, but Emma had had few relationships that really lasted when she was allowed to be fully honest about who she was. Even now, people tended to be so impressed by her family's social status that they focused on that instead of who she was as a person. And with social media making the world smaller, it didn't seem to matter when she was in another state. Her parents' society life still impacted her daily. Or at least it felt like it did. It wasn't that people disliked her when they found out. They just treated her differently.

"It's my family's. Did you want to talk about what else Noah said?"

Was that an edge in Kate's voice? Did she not want to be working at the lodge? Emma felt her curiosity building. But it wasn't really her business. She was only here for a short time.

Maybe extremely short. She planned to ask Noah in the morning if there was somewhere else she and Luke should go. She hated knowing other people were in danger because of her and she felt like Tyler was more upset than even she'd anticipated at their being there.

"Yes, please." She swallowed her feelings, tried to steady her expression so she'd be more put together. Inoffensive.

Her high-society parents would be proud of the face she was able to put on, the mask she was able to use, even in a situation like this. They'd taught her well, her entire life. Only Tyler had ever seen behind that mask...

And in the end he'd just asked too much of her, asked her to change too much of herself when she'd just been discovering who she was apart from her parents' expectations and rules.

"...bullet casings..."

Oops. Kate had been talking and Emma had been lost in her thoughts. She'd always been too much of a dreamer. "I'm sorry, Kate, what was the first part?"

"Noah found a couple of bullet casings. He's going to see if there are any prints on them that could help us. But besides that, we didn't learn too much."

"You're too humble for your own good, Kate."

Noah had walked in. He looked at Emma. "We also have a better idea of who is after you."

She widened her eyes, opened her mouth to ask for more details and then noticed Luke was stirring slightly. Noah must have noticed when her gaze went to him, though, because he stopped talking.

"Why don't we get you back to bed in our room, sweetheart? Everything is okay for now." She kept her voice even, comforting. Luke didn't fight her at all, just went willingly to her arms—though he was getting harder to hold at over sixty pounds, but Emma's arms had been toned by years of carrying him around as a baby and toddler. She'd been told she was spoiling her son by giving him so much attention, but she guessed she'd just always felt guilty about the fact that he had one parent less than he should and she'd decided she'd rather spoil him than not.

"I can carry him." Tyler spoke up. She hadn't even noticed him enter behind Noah.

And then it was hard to breathe again. Emma met his eyes, so much like Luke's, and bit her lip. Did she let him? Would Luke let him?

Luke reached out his arms and Emma let Tyler take him. "I like you," he said to Tyler as he settled his head on Tyler's shoulder. It hadn't been too many years since she'd had her head tucked against that shoulder, also. It was recent enough that she could still picture how it felt, firm, reassuring, like he could handle the weight of every care she'd ever carried.

Even though it was a result of her own choices that she'd never feel the solidness of his chest beneath her head again, it still hurt. So many regrets she couldn't do anything about now. Emma took a deep breath. She just needed to fully convince herself to move on, to acknowledge that Tyler's trust in her had been shattered to a degree that he could never have any kind of relationship with her again, probably not even friendship.

Of course, she realized now that since Tyler knew about Luke they'd have to see each other. Tyler was a good man, trustworthy, patient, made to be a dad. He'd want time with his son and while Emma had no idea how they'd work that out, she hoped they would somehow.

Tyler moved past her, holding Luke in his big, strong arms, and she hesitated for a second before following him. She didn't doubt that he had everything under control, and Luke was so enthralled by the attention, especially since he'd always known a man named Tyler Dawson was his dad and here he was in real life. But Emma had raised him on her own for seven years, had tucked him in every single night of his life. She wasn't going to stop any of that now. Some things might be changing, but others were very much staying the same.

Still, she tried to stay out of the way as much as possible, just watching what Tyler did.

He paused by the bed, as though trying to decide the best way to maneuver her son. He finally tightened one arm around Luke, who looked like he might have fallen asleep in his arms, and with the other arm pulled the covers back enough that he could settle Luke into them. Then with exquisite gentleness and kindness he pulled the covers up. Tucked his son in.

Emma watched as he ran a hand over Luke's forehead, brushing his bangs to the side. It so mirrored what she did when she tucked him in, but it was Tyler. She swallowed hard.

He turned, looked startled at her presence. "Didn't think I could handle it?" Did he mean putting Luke to bed tonight? Or the fact that she'd kept all this from him?

"I knew you could."

Tyler stepped toward her, his broad, muscular frame seeming even larger in the small, dark room. Her heartbeat sped up, breathing quickened. How could his *presence* affect her so much? It had been years, shouldn't any lingering emotions have completely dissipated by now?

"I don't just mean tonight." His voice was rough around the edges, scratchy from the late-night hours.

"I know."

"We didn't get to finish our conversation."

"And you want to now?" Emma wished she could take the words back as soon as she said them, because the look of incredulity on Tyler's face said it all. She'd kept his son a secret for over half a decade and *she* had the nerve to act like she was inconvenienced by him wanting to talk?

"Let me kiss him good-night." She moved to Luke's side, kissed the forehead Tyler had touched just minutes before, her heart squeezing with love for her son. "Can one of your siblings sit with him in here? Just to make sure he's safe until we're...done talking?"

Tyler nodded, left the room and came back with Kate, who didn't ask anything, just settled into the chair in the corner of the room. "I'm not sleepy. You guys take your time."

Emma followed Tyler out of the room. They walked down the hallway silently, Emma not sure where they were heading. He finally pushed open a heavy door toward the end of the hallway. His bedroom? Emma didn't want that, didn't want to see where he lived, in such a personal way. She needed to think of him as an…acquaintance. A possible future partner in child raising. Something along those lines if she wanted her heart to survive without being more damaged than it already was.

Not that she blamed Tyler. Not anymore.

He wanted to know why she hadn't told him. And she didn't know what to say. Her reasons had changed over the years, as she had, and then finally, eventually, there had been no reason at all. Just inertia. Her own fear.

Hardly a good excuse for keeping him in the dark about something so important. If only she could go back and change her choices…

"It's the media room." Tyler held the door open for her. She tried to school her expression, assuming she must have made some face that reflected her apprehension that it was his room.

Nodding, she went inside the dark, windowless room. She appreciated the privacy, even if she did feel pressure to explain something that was completely unexplainable at this point.

"Sit anywhere you'll be comfortable."

That was Tyler. Always the gentleman. He may be angrier at her than he'd ever been at anyone in his life, but he was still polite, still caring. Emma chose a couch, wasn't surprised when Tyler took the other end of it. She appreciated his closeness—it would mean she could at least talk quietly, wouldn't have to broadcast her mistakes loudly enough that someone walking by would hear them.

"First. Tyler, I'm sorry."

She looked up at him. He met her eyes and, for half a second, there wasn't eight years between their breakup and this moment.

He was just Tyler.

Emma wanted to stay quiet, wanted to just stay in the moment. But she couldn't. She'd made her choices. And now she had to live with them.

Emma's eyes were full of pain, something Tyler hadn't expected. He'd never actually known anyone who kept a baby a secret from the father. And he wasn't proud to admit it, but he'd formed all sorts of unfair judgments about this new version of Emma because of that. But maybe she wasn't a new version, just an older one of the one he'd loved before.

She looked away from him and he watched as she swallowed hard, appeared to gather her composure. He waited, not sure how much more waiting he could take.

"I couldn't be who you wanted, Tyler."

"That doesn't explain why you would keep my *son* a secret from me."

Emma winced like he'd struck her on the word *son*. She nodded. "I know it seems that way, but please, let me explain."

Tyler didn't say anything. Just waited.

"I wasn't…as sure of myself as it seemed in college."

Tyler thought she seemed to be choosing her words carefully. It was a well-thought-out explanation but not rehearsed. Somehow he appreciated that, like there was a greater chance she was giving him the whole truth and not just a variation of it.

Of course, when they'd been together he'd never had a reason to doubt her honesty. She'd always been herself with him, always been upfront. Or so he'd thought.

"I knew I couldn't be who you wanted when you said you were going back to Alaska. I couldn't be that brave outdoorsy woman who followed you to the ends of the earth. I was raised differently."

"You never said much about how you grew up." He'd put the pieces together, though. She'd come to school in a brand new BMW, never had to worry about how often she went out to eat, always dressed well.

There went that mask over her face again, the one he'd noticed in college when he'd tried to talk about her upbringing. He'd thought the two of them were close at the time—they had obviously been close enough to make a child together and neither of them were into casual relationships—but there had been big parts of herself that Emma had held back from him.

Suddenly he stopped seeing her as the one who had done the hurting, saw how maybe she'd been acting from a place of hurt. His chest tightened as he thought of the little boy down the hall, the one whose birth he'd missed. The one whose *everything* he'd missed.

And his own walls were up once more.

"I grew up in Dallas. My family had a lot of money and a lot of ideas as to how we should all look, act and behave at all times."

"Okay, so?"

Her mask cracked, anguish glimmered in her eyes. "I didn't know how to be anyone other than who people wanted me to be, Tyler. I'm sorry…it's my fault I wasn't stronger, my fault I didn't understand. You want to know the real reason I broke up with you? It's because I was sitting in the bathroom in my apartment, staring at a stick with two pink lines and re-alizing that I was going to be responsible for raising another human and I didn't even know who I was." She sighed. "That sounds wrong. I just... I wanted to not be stuck being someone I wasn't for the rest of my life. I knew you'd do the right thing, knew you'd insist we get married whether you really wanted to or not, but I couldn't do Alaska, Tyler. I'm not some backwoods girl who chops firewood and can skin a deer."

"We don't have deer on the Kenai Peninsula."

"Moose, then." She shook her head. "I knew you and I couldn't work, not because of you but because of me, and I didn't want to do that to us."

"So you just left."

"I left."

"And kept Luke a secret."

Emma swallowed hard. "I meant to tell you. I thought I'd wait, make sure the pregnancy went okay."

"Did you want...?"

"Stop. I wanted him, Tyler. I wanted him from the second I knew he existed. I just didn't want to rock your whole world if something was going to go wrong anyway."

"He still would have been my son, Emma. I still deserved to know."

"You did. And I should have told you. I meant to... I meant to before I went into labor. I meant to that first Christmas, his first birthday, every holiday and birthday after that. I have a shoebox full of letters I wrote you, talking about Luke and how he was growing up, pages filled with me trying to explain, trying to say I was sorry." She was talking with her hands now, like she did when she was passionate about something.

She shook her head. "I should have told you."

Heartbeats passed, gave space for his thoughts, the emotions he couldn't begin to identify that were swirling around inside him. "You told me now, though. You came here now." The thought had really only just occurred to him, had only just fully formed.

"I did."

"Why?"

"Because I knew I could count on you. I-if someone is after me... if something happens to me... I need to know Luke is safe and taken care of."

"I'm surprised you didn't just go to your parents."

Her expression shuttered. "If you think that, you weren't listening to anything I said. They don't— They wanted…" She trailed off, shook her head like she could shake the negative thoughts away. "This wasn't their plan for me."

Tyler couldn't comprehend how anyone could look at that child and not understand that while human mistakes might have been made, his birth, his creation, hadn't been one of them. That boy was a gift from God. A sudden protectiveness rose within him, shock at the fact anyone might not view him that way.

In a way, he felt like he was looking at Emma with new eyes, like he'd been missing a piece of who she was not knowing how she'd been raised. But this detail told him a lot. Maybe more than he wanted to know.

"Don't look at me like that, Tyler. Don't feel sorry for me. I still should have told you— nothing excuses that—and I just want you to know that I get that. I get that what I did, keeping him from you, is unforgivable." Words tumbled from her lips now, as though a dam had burst and taken her filters with it.

Now that Tyler thought about it in light of what he'd just learned, Emma had always been careful to present herself the way she wanted people to see her. But she wasn't doing that now. She was hitting him full-force, nothing held back, all Emma.

He braced himself against feelings, both unwelcome and unidentifiable, and listened.

"So while I'd love to have your forgiveness, I'm not asking for it. I think it's too much to ask for and all I want from you, Tyler, though you don't owe me this, either, is for you to help me keep our son safe." She paused, almost gasped for breath in the quick break from the words. "And if I can't take care of him anymore, if something happens to me—"

"I'm not going to let it."

The look she gave him was anguish and agony. "Tyler."

"I'm serious, Emma."

"So am I. I need to know you'll keep him. Love him. Accept him even though…"

"What you did—anything that's transpired between you and me—has nothing to do with Luke."

Emma started and, for a second, Tyler wondered if his tone had been too harsh. He hadn't intended to sound cruel, had only intended to firmly get it into her head that Luke was his son, too, and he'd always, from this moment on, treat him as such.

She met his eyes. "Okay."

"Okay?"

She took a deep breath, stuck out a hand,

almost drew her fingers back, but then took another breath and left it out there, extended toward him. "Truce?"

He wanted to call it so much more than that. Wanted to rewind the clock, change the past—all things that were impossible. But he couldn't do any of those things so instead he stuck out his hand, shook hers, and was every bit as affected by her touch as he'd expected, though he tried his best not to let it show.

"Truce."

SIX

Morning came too quickly for Emma, who felt like she'd tossed and turned all night. So much had changed since she'd witnessed the murder in Dallas. Had it really only been a couple of weeks?

Despite her lack of sleep she felt more clear-headed than she had since she'd arrived in Alaska, specifically at Moose Haven Lodge. The conversation with Tyler had gone as well as a soul-bearing, awful conversation like that could have gone. She felt too vulnerable, embarrassed, grateful and at least five other emotions she'd have had trouble naming, but at least it was over. Now they could move on, find their new normal. Or…well, figure out who wanted her dead and then work on those other things.

Emma checked on Luke, who was sleeping soundly next to her, and then moved quietly to the bathroom where she showered and changed into clothes Kate had left her. She was thankful they were the same size, though Emma usually dressed in pastels and it was clear that wasn't Kate's style. Still, the blue jeans and black long-sleeved Henley were comfortable, warm, and clean, and Emma was thankful for them. She still hadn't had the chance to ask Noah about their belongings but needed to do that today.

When she finished getting ready, Luke was just starting to stir.

"Morning, munchkin." She smiled at him. "You ready for breakfast?"

His sleepy morning frown eased into a hopeful look. "Do you think they have pancakes? I had a dream about pancakes last night." He rubbed his pajama-covered tummy in an exaggerated gesture of hunger.

Emma smiled indulgently. "I think there's a pretty good chance we can find pancakes." If they didn't serve them to the lodge guests, Emma figured she could just borrow a little corner of the Dawsons' private kitchen to make some. She wasn't the best in the kitchen, but she had the world's best pancake recipe, at least in her opinion. She'd learned it in college, though at the moment she couldn't remember who had taught her. Maybe her junior year roommate, Amy?

"Yay!" Luke threw the covers back and pulled on his clothes from yesterday. Emma winced. He was at that age where if he ran around enough he smelled...well, very much like a boy, and it was her opinion that his clothes couldn't be worn twice because of that.

Then again, her car and all its contents were in Anchorage, being processed by the troopers. So maybe beggars couldn't be choosers.

Still, she made a mental note to figure out how to get into downtown Moose Haven today. Surely there was a shop that had kids' clothes of some kind. While Noah and Tyler hadn't thought to grab her bags from the scene of the wreck as far as she knew, they'd met her at the hospital with her purse.

They headed down the stairs together, Emma feeling more normal than she had in days.

Until she saw Tyler at the bottom of the stairs. He wasn't watching her, he was watching Luke, a look on his face that made her chest clench. How could he love Luke so much already? Emma had no idea, but it was clear that he did.

"Hey, buddy. Did you sleep well?" He held

out a fist for a fist bump, which Luke happily gave him.

"I slept great! I dreamed about pancakes and my mom said I could have some if we could find some."

"I said I'd see what I could do," she corrected, feeling a slight blush on her cheeks. She didn't want Tyler to think she was making herself *too* at home here, but she wanted her son to feel as settled as possible during this crazy time in his life.

"I'll make pancakes." Tyler bent to Luke's level. "I make the best pancakes."

"No, my mom does."

Tyler's eyebrows raised and Emma remembered where she'd gotten that recipe. *Ohhh.* She smiled slightly. "It's your recipe." She shrugged. "You do make the best pancakes."

He held her gaze and a few seconds passed. Emma's heart beat a crazy rhythm in her chest, one that made it hard to catch her breath, but then Tyler looked away and everything returned to normal so quickly she almost wondered if she'd imagined…whatever it was.

She followed the two of them down the stairs, noticing for the first time how much they looked alike, even from the back. She'd noticed the eyes, of course, as soon as Luke's eyes had shifted when he was a toddler from a dark blue to mossy green. Those were Tyler's eyes. The rest? She didn't know if she hadn't looked for it or if she'd intentionally tried not to notice how much her son shared with the man she'd once loved.

Emma followed them to the kitchen and would have helped with the pancake prep, but it was obvious Tyler had both it and Luke under control. Instead she wandered back into the Dawsons' living room in search of a notepad and a pen. She woken with questions about the case, things she wanted answers to as quickly as possible, and she wanted to write them down before she forgot.

She finally found what she needed in a desk drawer next to a chair that sat in a corner by the window. As she pulled out the writing tools, the outside caught her attention. The lodge sat in a clearing with rocks at the edge, and today the trees seemed to be even brighter orange and gold than yesterday. Fall was coming to Alaska full-force. But unlike yesterday's clear, blue sky, today's was covered by a thick layer of low-hanging clouds.

Emma could feel the uncertainty in the air, to such a degree she wondered if it meant some kind of storm was coming or if it really was just a mirror of how she felt. Something told her to move away from the window—likely common sense—but she couldn't stop staring. Someone had been out there last night, probably the same someone who had killed her boss, or at least someone involved with whoever the murderer had been. Was there one suspect or a group of them? It was one of the questions she had, one she needed to write down.

"You shouldn't stand so close to the window."

Emma jumped as her heart skipped a beat, though she realized as soon as she did that the voice belonged to Noah. She looked up at him, let out a breath. "You're right. I was just thinking that, but I couldn't help it."

"It's a lot to take in, isn't it? Everything that has happened to you lately."

Emma nodded. "I'm not used to someone being after me, to thinking about people wanting to commit crimes, things like that. I don't know how guys like you do it."

He shrugged. It didn't surprise her that Tyler's family members were as modest about their skills as he was. Emma had been raised to flaunt her skills, be proud of them. It wasn't that the Dawsons seemed self-deprecating by any means. Rather, they seemed to be confident enough in their skills that they didn't need to seek praise for them. Was that something that was just part of who they were, or was it because of their faith in Jesus, because of something in the Bible she hadn't learned yet?

Emma hadn't become a Christian until after everything had happened with Tyler. That was something she'd like to tell him about if she ever got the chance, to thank him for. They might have made some mistakes, but Tyler had had a genuine faith, and he'd taught her a lot, opened her eyes to the truth about God and God's desire to have a relationship with her.

She hadn't been willing to listen then, had still felt like she had things pretty together on her own. It hadn't taken long after her life had started to fall apart for her to realize that she'd always needed God. Everyone did.

Another thing about Luke's birth that she could be thankful for. She couldn't have made it through the last eight years without Jesus.

"So what's next, Noah? What are you guys doing?" She realized immediately it sounded like she was questioning their skills, which hadn't been her intention at all. "I didn't mean it the way it came out," she hurried to explain.

Noah shook his head. "No worries. I get that you were just asking. I'll admit we don't have as much to go on as I'd like right now. I'll probably try to get in touch with whoever has the case in Dallas…"

"I think the Texas DPS CID might be involved by this point but it started out with the Dallas police department." Emma almost laughed at how easily the acronyms she'd never heard until recently came out of her mouth. The Department of Public Safety's Criminal Investigations Division was the next level up from the regular police department.

He nodded. "All right, so I'll start with them. I'll also be keeping in close contact with the troopers about this. On a practical level here on the ground, we were able to get some shell casings from the area where you were shot at last night. I'd be surprised if those came back with prints, but we do know that the gun they were using is a .270 rifle. Kate was also able to give us some estimates about the size of the suspect."

"What about me? What can I be doing?"

"Staying safe." The words came without hesitation, with no consideration of what she was asking, and Emma fought a wave of frustration. She'd spent the last eight years taking care of herself and while some small part of her could appreciate that the Dawsons wanted her to stay alive—more than a small part of her, really—she also wanted to help, not just be left on the sidelines. She'd never lived her life like a victim and she didn't intend to start now.

"What else?" She hoped her tone made it clear she wasn't taking "nothing" as a valid answer. There had to be something she could do from the safety of the lodge that could help with the investigation somehow.

"Let me think on it, okay?"

It was better than "nothing" and she felt like Noah meant it, like he was really going to consider it and let her know. Emma nodded. "Okay, keep me posted."

"I promise." Emma let his voice reassure her. "And for now, stay away from windows. Also, I was able to get your suitcases out of evidence. They're out in my car but I'll bring them in and put them in your room later."

She felt her shoulders relax slightly. One less worry. "Thanks, Noah."

Emma stepped away from the window and headed off to join Tyler and Luke. It was so hard to get it to sink into her mind that though things were changing in some ways for the better—she was about to join her son and his *dad* for breakfast—she had to be alert at all times. She couldn't let her guard down even for a minute because someone out there wanted her dead. And Emma knew he wouldn't stop until he'd succeeded.

Or until someone managed to stop him.

Tyler couldn't get over what his life had turned out to be this week. This morning he'd been sitting in the kitchen, eating pancakes with his son and Emma Bass. He still needed to talk to her to find out when she was going to let him tell Luke. So far the kid had been affectionate with him, but for all Tyler knew he was like that with everyone. He hadn't addressed Tyler directly yet, but hearing him call him by his first name, or worse, "Mr. Dawson," would hurt. Would Emma mind if Luke called him "Dad"?

The longer she was there, the longer *they* were there, the more unanswered questions Tyler had.

For now, Summer and Kate had volunteered to spend the day with Luke. So far, since the car accident, he hadn't been in any more danger, but they weren't taking chances and were sticking pretty close to the lodge, though Tyler had heard one of his sisters promise a trip outside to the chicken pen to see the chickens. Moose Haven Lodge took the whole farm-to-table concept seriously; it had been something his parents had done before it was fashionable and Tyler tried to keep up the tradition. They got most of their meat and vegetables from either local farmers on the Kenai Peninsula or up in Palmer, and they raised their own chickens for eggs. Since the lodge was most well known for its breakfast, they really could never have too many eggs.

Emma had excused herself to her room after kissing Luke goodbye and telling him to have fun. His heartbeat quickening, Tyler hurried up the stairs to her room, not sure what exactly he was going to say but knowing that Noah had told him to keep her safe. Even if he hadn't, Tyler wouldn't have been able to trust anyone else to do the job. She might not be *his* anymore…but he felt responsible for her anyway.

He still wasn't sure what to do with any of these feelings, though he had a pretty good idea what Emma would say if he admitted he felt like she needed his protection to stay safe. She'd been independent years ago, and he was fairly certain she wouldn't have grown less so in the intervening years when she'd been raising a boy by herself.

Tyler knocked on the door. Waited.

Emma opened it and instead of looking surprised to see him, she ushered him in. "I just have to grab a couple more things."

She looked incredible, her hair perfect with shiny brown waves that framed her face. Did she have any idea how beautiful she was? Tyler shoved the thought from his mind as soon as it materialized. He certainly didn't need to have any thoughts about that, but nothing had stopped that one from popping into his mind, had it?

"Going somewhere?"

"You and I are going to the library in town."

He quirked a brow. "And why's that?"

"Research. Lists. Helping with the case… Try to keep up, Tyler."

"Does Noah know about this?"

"It was his idea."

Somehow Tyler doubted that. He didn't doubt that Noah had said *something*; Emma wasn't a liar. But he was pretty sure his brother hadn't given a woman in danger an assignment to go into town on some kind of fact-finding mission and he was even more certain that he wouldn't have implied that the Moose Haven PD needed any help solving the case on its own. Noah had been the chief for years and he was proud of his department, small though it was. In fact, there was a constant tension between Noah and Trooper Erynn Cooper, the one trooper stationed in Moose Haven, because Noah didn't like sharing his investigations.

"Why don't we do your research here? We have computers, backwoods though a little Alaskan lodge is bound to be." He couldn't help the last bit of sarcasm. Okay, he could have, but he hadn't wanted to. *Backwoods* was one of the words Emma had used years ago when she'd told him all the reasons why she couldn't go to Alaska with him, saying she couldn't be with him because their dreams were in different places.

She flinched and Tyler sensed his words finding their mark, though it gave him less satisfaction than he'd anticipated.

"I can only say I'm sorry so many times, Tyler."

Had she said she was sorry for leaving him or just for not telling him about Luke? Then again, maybe it was all connected in her mind. Tyler couldn't know that, but he knew he needed to let the past go. Not forget it, because he had no intention of repeating any of it, which was why acknowledging any lingering attraction to Emma wasn't going to do either of them any good. Because he *wouldn't* act on it this time, not in any way, and he wasn't going to get hurt again.

He met her eyes.

Wasn't going to let her get hurt again, either.

"Tell me why you think we should go to the library." He decided to take another tactic. Kindness, treating her like a capable adult. It was worth a try and maybe it would help keep any inclination for sarcasm in check.

"I've already been attacked here, Tyler, so we know whoever is after me doesn't care where I am."

"That makes sense but, if anything, that's an argument for staying here. We've got home court advantage."

She lifted her chin. "We've also got a big crowd if we're at the library. People will see us."

"You want whoever is after you to see you, don't you? To see you investigating?" Tyler didn't know where the realization had even come from but he was fairly certain he was right.

Emma shrugged. "Maybe. I don't want to be a victim."

"Sure, but acting all empowered and putting yourself in danger doesn't make you less of a victim."

"It *does*, Tyler." She pushed past him through the door. "But I wouldn't expect you to understand."

Tyler didn't see any real reason he shouldn't go along with her plan, so he followed her to his car and they climbed in.

He kept a close eye on the rearview mirror during the entire drive to town. He wouldn't be surprised if whoever was after her followed them. Had they been at the lodge since the shooting last night, waiting? That was a question he hadn't considered, but he supposed it was possible. He needed to talk to Noah today, to get a better idea of what his brother thought they might be dealing with. Tyler may have had all the information from his police academy classes fresh on his mind, but Noah had experience on his side, and more intuition than Tyler felt he possessed. His brother would know what to do.

They made it to town without incident and Tyler parked in front of the library, looking around for anything that looked out of place.

"Maybe this wasn't such a good idea." Emma's voice was soft. Unsteady.

Tyler looked in her direction, noted the way she seemed to have paled. He could see why—Moose Haven was a small town but the downtown area was wide open. From the library parking lot he could see the softball fields, the coffee shop, several restaurants, the dock… there were so many places for a sniper to hide. Although just because they'd found a sniper-caliber shell last night didn't mean the person after Emma was good enough to be an actual sniper. In fact, if Tyler listened to *his* instincts, it wasn't someone sniper trained. Otherwise the shooter wouldn't have missed.

More likely, in his opinion, it was someone completely amateur, who was relying on crime shows and internet searches for ideas on how to eliminate someone.

He should mention those thoughts to Noah, see what he thought. For now, however, he needed to reassure Emma, because if she'd become less sure of her idea, he'd grown more certain that venturing out now and then like this was better than essentially holding her hostage in the lodge. There was danger everywhere, but for now nothing merited locking her away. And in addition to whatever computer research Emma had in mind, Tyler thought they could talk to some of the towns-people in Moose Haven, see if anyone had noticed anything suspicious that could help them with the case.

"I think we'll be okay."

She still looked unconvinced. Without thinking or considering the consequences, Tyler took her hand and squeezed it gently. Her skin was warm beneath his, her hand so achingly familiar it was as if he felt a jolt of electricity pass between them.

He'd meant to reassure her, give her confidence. Instead he'd shaken his own.

Tyler released her hand slowly, hoping he didn't give away how much the small moment had shaken him.

They climbed from the car without another word and he was left guessing what she was thinking, left reminding himself that, when it came down to it, she could trust him.

But Tyler couldn't trust her. And that wasn't going to change. They might have a past, electricity, all of it. But none of that meant they had a future.

SEVEN

Emma exhaled a deep sigh when they made it into the library without incident. She wasn't sure what she'd been thinking this morning when this had sounded like such a good idea, but she'd been second-guessing it ever since. Not even the knowledge that Tyler now seemed to be on board with their public outing did much to help, which surprised her since at one time his judgments and opinions had meant a lot to her.

At the moment, her sense of disquiet was so great, the pit in her stomach ever present, that not much could reassure her. It had been a few weeks since she'd witnessed the murder in Dallas. She'd called the police department this morning, but they hadn't been able to give her much information other than what she'd read in the paper. It was now being called a homicide. Suspect at large. Motive unknown.

Collateral damage? Also unknown because she couldn't seem to get anyone at the police department to take seriously the fact that someone was after her now. That wasn't fair, she realized as soon as she thought it. They might be taking her seriously, but they weren't able to protect her and that had been reason enough to leave. At least whoever was after her hadn't threatened Luke directly. Having someone after her affected him greatly, of course. But his safety didn't seem to be in question and, for that, she was thankful.

"Where did you want to start?"

Emma swallowed hard, willing herself not to have the slightest reaction to Tyler's deep voice so close to her ear. "I want to figure out who was after my boss and who's after me."

"That's what we all want." He chuckled, the sound so foreign she stared at him. She'd noticed he was different, but hadn't been able to articulate why. But she hadn't heard him laugh in the two days she'd been in Moose Haven, not till now. True, circumstances hadn't been anything close to lighthearted, but Tyler hadn't been so uptight in college, had he?

"Where should we start to figure that out?"

He'd been talking and she hadn't heard him. Emma tuned back in. "I think we should look into the company where I worked, see if they were having money trouble, things like that. I noticed some things in some papers I was filing right before…"

He held up his index finger, motioned for her to wait. "Computers are this way." A shiver went through her as she looked around at the other patrons as she followed Tyler. Everyone looked involved in what they were doing, but appearances could be deceiving, couldn't they? Was her attacker here, listening? Chills ran up her spine. Would someone attack her here even with witnesses? She had no idea, had no kind of training that would allow her to make even a moderately educated guess.

Emma followed Tyler across the quiet library, not able to decide if she appreciated that he was letting her take the lead on this or not. Hadn't she just gotten upset with Noah because he *wouldn't* let her help? So, what? Did she want Noah to treat her like a capable woman and Tyler to protect her like the damsel in distress she was but would really rather not be? Her feelings were awhirl inside her, blending together in such a way that it was impossible to identify half of them. All she knew was that she needed to stop letting her emotions dictate what she did because she had a case to solve and a life to save—hers.

Tyler slowed as he came up to the computers, then motioned for her to follow him. They settled in a spot she suspected he'd chosen because of the fact that it was in a corner, two walls behind them so no one could come near them without being seen. Emma appreciated his consideration. Maybe it was okay being taken care of after all.

"So you noticed what exactly in the papers?" he asked quietly from his seat beside her. He'd let her take the one directly in front of the computer, once again making it clear that she was in charge here.

Emma thought back to her last week of work in the office, shrugged her shoulders and sighed. "Not much, really. Just enough that I was going to talk to my boss about it that night."

"Was staying late that night unusual?"

She shook her head. "No, I worked late every Tuesday and Thursday."

"Why?"

She shrugged. "Good work ethic?" A desire to prove that she was valuable to the company, to make sure she was promoted if the opportunity ever came? She didn't want to remind

Tyler of her lie of omission in not telling him about Luke, so she didn't bring him up, but she was a single mom. She worked hard and long.

"So what was it specifically that caught your eye?"

"Money being moved to an account that wasn't named with a project name that was familiar to me."

"Any chance it could have been something legit that you just weren't aware of yet?"

She nodded. "Yes, actually." It was all she'd had to go on so far, and while she'd liked her boss and certainly didn't want to believe the worst of him, especially now that he was dead, if this lead didn't pan out, they had nothing. Unless there was some kind of evidence in her car, which she doubted. Not that she had any reason to doubt other than a newfound pessimistic nature.

"You're frowning again. You've done that a lot." Tyler's observation was innocent enough but, coupled with the thoughts she was having now, it darkened Emma's sprits even more.

Some days she wondered what had happened to the carefree woman she used to be, but she didn't *really* wonder. She knew exactly what had happened to her. She'd grown up. Didn't growing up mean getting more serious? Or had she abandoned too much of her personality after college, after Tyler?

She chose to ignore Tyler's comment. At least, not give it a verbal response. Instead she steered the conversation away from her mood, which she certainly didn't want to ponder anymore, and back to the case.

"If this account was legit…" She stared at the computer where she'd pulled up her former company's website, more for inspiration than anything else, though she was planning to log into her account to see if there were any files that could help them solve this puzzle. "If it was legit, then I can't come up with any reason someone would be after my boss."

"Hey." He moved his hand toward her arm then jerked it back. She swallowed hard, just as shaken up as if he'd actually touched her. She understood the instinctive reaction to reassure someone with touch, but she understood equally why he hadn't followed through. That brief time he'd held her hand in the car must have been enough for both of them.

It had certainly been enough for her.

"What?" She made herself meet his eyes,

trying not to notice their color, which she'd once found herself getting lost in all too often.

"Don't get discouraged. We'll figure this out."

"Not to put a damper on your newfound optimism," Emma began, feeling herself getting more frustrated by the minute, "but I'm a marketing specialist and you run an inn. Really, unless Noah finds something, we probably can't do much." She shrugged. "I don't know why I thought I could."

He raised his eyebrows at her, his expression changing like he knew something she didn't know.

"What?"

He didn't answer.

"Tyler. What?"

"Were you really trusting me to protect you, thinking that I'm just some guy with a gun and good intentions?"

Emma swallowed hard, feeling a blush rise slightly on her cheeks as she shrugged. "Maybe."

"I've been gone from Moose Haven for weeks, up until a couple of weeks ago. I've been in Sitka, at the police academy, in case Noah needed extra help."

"The *police academy*?" Her traitorous mind pictured Tyler, his face, his broad, muscular shoulders, but in a police uniform. She quickly blocked the image from her mind. It wasn't helpful, to say the least, in her quest to feel nothing for him.

He nodded.

"So…" She finished putting the pieces together. "You might actually know what we're looking for."

He laughed. *Again.* Since when was Tyler the relaxed one in comparison to Emma? Then again, he didn't have anyone after him, now did he?

She frowned.

"Hey, I'm not laughing at you. I'm just glad I did the academy. It seemed a little crazy at the time but Noah asked me to, and he's family, so I went for it." He shrugged. "Now it's proving even more worthwhile."

More so than helping family? But no, she couldn't let herself read into everything he said like that.

"Let's get started then."

Emma logged into her account, hope starting to win the battle inside her. Maybe there was something they could do, after all, something they could find. She had access to the files she'd questioned from here. If Tyler could look at them and decide if they might be a motive for someone killing her boss, they might be able to start compiling a list of people who could have murdered him, who could be after her.

They were making progress—or so she'd thought—and then her newfound optimism started to dwindle.

Two hours later and nothing in the files looked noteworthy to Tyler.

"This was a dumb idea, wasn't it?" Emma rubbed her forehead at the temples where a headache was starting to build. Why had she been so sure she'd found evidence of wrongdoing? It had looked so suspicious in Dallas, but here, with Tyler's trained opinion telling her there was nothing out of the ordinary, she didn't know what she'd been thinking. It was clear the "suspicious" account she'd seen was nothing more than an account she hadn't known the name of. Unless there was something they were missing, Mike and the company had been completely on the up and up.

But if her boss hadn't been murdered because of something at work, why was he dead? He'd been in his midforties. Single. Not into the party scene or anything else. He'd led a fairly boring life as far as Emma could tell.

"So what now? Should we just go home?" Emma's eyes widened and her breath caught. "Your home. The lodge. Not my home. I only meant—"

"I knew what you meant, Emma. Calm down." He smiled a little. "And no, it wasn't a dumb idea…and we aren't going home yet. I'm going to call the Dallas police, just to make sure there aren't any other leads we can look into while we're here. Then I think we should talk to people."

"Which people?"

"Townspeople."

"Here in Moose Haven?" Emma furrowed her brow. "What would they know about this?"

The tenderness that had been on his face moments before was gone as quickly as it had come. In its place was the guarded-looking Tyler. "We may be pretty backwoods, Emma, but people do notice things. Whoever wants you dead has been here and I want to know if anyone detected anything suspicious."

"I didn't mean—"

He shook his head. "I know what you think of the town. You don't have to try to explain.

I'm going to step into the lobby and call Dallas. I won't be out of sight."

Tyler strode off.

Emma sighed, exhaled and relaxed against the back of the chair. She hadn't realized how much the last couple hours of one-on-one time with Tyler had affected her, but every muscle in her shoulders ached. She closed her eyes for a second, wishing he hadn't misunderstood her last comment, wishing the last decade had been different, wishing she didn't have so many things she wished she could change.

A shiver moved over her shoulders and Emma felt cold. She opened her eyes.

Someone was watching her.

Tyler hung up the phone, then looked back into the library where Emma sat waiting. Her eyes were closed and she looked relaxed. He smiled a little, old feelings stirring, but he pushed them away. No matter what he did, what *they* did, he was always going to feel like he couldn't measure up to some invisible standard Emma had because he was from Moose Haven. It was part of him, this silly small town, and he was tired of feeling like she wanted him to apologize for it.

His frustration wavered for a second. *She*

had come *here*. Was it possible her long-ago thoughts weren't valid anymore, didn't reflect what she really thought, and he'd overreacted to her comment just now?

He should ask. They weren't going to get anywhere refusing to communicate and for Luke's sake they had to maintain some kind of relationship.

He glanced back at Emma.

The change in her had him hurrying back inside. She was sitting up now, straight and tall, eyes wide open. The posture of someone who'd been threatened. What had happened?

"Tyler! There you are! I've been meaning to ask you something." Mrs. Brown, the world's sweetest librarian, placed a hand on his shoulder as soon as he entered the building again. He smiled at her but shook his head. "I'm sorry, I've got to get back to my...friend for a minute."

Not caring if it seemed rude, which was completely unlike him, he kept his eyes focused on Emma, her own eyes darting around the library. What had happened? What had he missed? He'd looked away for—what?—maybe half a minute at most. Not even that long.

She'd noticed something though.

"What is it?" he asked as soon as he was within earshot.

Emma shook her head. "I don't know."

"You saw someone?"

"No."

He reached out, rested a hand on her shoulder, needing the physical contact to reassure himself she was there, in person, and still okay.

Had he cared this much for her the entire time they'd been apart? The question wormed its way into his mind, put there by the reaction to his touching her. Tyler didn't know. Yes. Probably. But caring about someone didn't mean the relationship was right. And his and Emma's wasn't.

He swallowed hard, moved his hand and tried to get hold of his emotions. His siblings teased him for being rock-solid, sometimes for being a stick in the mud. He was the least "fun" Dawson sibling, the one who took responsibilities the most seriously, who acted on his feelings less than anyone. What was it about Emma Bass that made all of that go out the window, made him want to just live without weighing all the consequences? There was something to be said for responsibility and Tyler, of all people, knew it. But at the same time...

She really made you happy once. Kate's words from earlier this morning echoed in his mind. She'd hijacked him when he'd been in the middle of making pancakes. Why his sister had felt the need to interfere, he had no idea. Summer was the hopeless romantic. If practical Kate was trying to give him relationship advice, Tyler didn't know what to do anymore.

"Let's go back to the lodge." He struggled to get the words out, to focus on the fact that something had Emma shaken. All he knew at this point was that the threat seemed to have passed. He didn't notice anything out of place, so it seemed okay to not take any drastic measures, but going back to the lodge for now couldn't be a bad idea. They could regroup and come back to town to talk to the residents another time.

"Okay."

It didn't feel right, not having her fight him or attempt to argue with his opinions. She was too quiet. What had happened?

They'd just pulled away from the library when she finally spoke.

"Someone was watching me."

"You're sure?"

"Yes."

He pulled the car over, made a U-turn.

"What are you doing?" Her voice had risen, both in pitch and volume.

"We've got to go back in there. What if the person who's after you is sitting there and we just let them get away because you got a little spooked and I overreacted?"

"A little spooked?" Who knew her voice could go higher? But it did.

"Take it easy, Emma, I'm not trying to be insulting."

"Sure you're not. Because you're Tyler. Perfect Tyler who never does anything wrong." Her voice broke off. "Fine. Whatever. Forget I said that, but I'm not going in there."

"Did I ever say I haven't made bad choices? I have, okay? I'm not perfect. What does that have to do with going back?"

"Just, please, take me back to the lodge."

He slowed the speed of the car slightly.

"Please."

Tyler stole a glance in her direction. She didn't look good. Well, she did. Too good. But she didn't look like she felt good. She looked about half a centimeter from the edge of breaking down. "Okay. We'll go home."

She didn't comment on his use of the word *home*. And Tyler was glad because he didn't want to admit that it was intentional. He wanted, if only for a few days, to pretend like she belonged in his life.

He swallowed hard and corrected himself, forcing the words out. "To the lodge, I mean." No matter how much he might want to, this was no time to pretend, no time to offer false hope. It was too late for them and he needed to focus on figuring out who wanted her dead so she could get out of his town and back out of his life, except for the occasional visits he hoped he'd be able to have with Luke. They hadn't exactly had the chance to talk about that yet.

Tyler pulled his cell phone out, dialed Noah's number.

"What's up?"

"Hey. Can you get to the library ASAP?"

"I'm next door at the post office, I'll head over now." Tyler could hear a door shutting in the background. "Okay, what am I looking for?"

"Just look at everyone who's there."

"It's pretty full, could I get more details?"

"Emma felt someone watching her." She was quiet now in the passenger seat, and Tyler didn't know what she thought about the fact that he'd called his brother. He'd needed to do something, though. They couldn't let a possible lead disappear, but he just couldn't make her go back in there. He'd never seen her quite so rattled.

"I'll see what I can find and let you know later. Keep her in sight, okay?"

"I will."

He set the phone down and kept driving, wondering if he was imagining the fact that Emma seemed to be relaxing slightly with every extra bit of distance he put between them and the library.

Tyler glanced in her direction. She was still tense. Because of what she said about him being perfect? Tyler couldn't begin to guess. He felt in some ways like he didn't know her anymore.

Then again, what if that was true? Was there a reason he could start getting to know her? He'd certainly be able to do a better job protecting her. He considered it for a minute, decided there was something to that.

"So, what should we do the rest of the day?" He chose to test the conversational waters with something inoffensive that couldn't possible spark any kind of upset.

"Seriously?" Her eyebrows raised.

Okay. He'd assumed it wouldn't cause any upheaval but it wasn't the first time he'd been wrong.

"Seriously what? Listen, we have to be together, Emma."

"Excuse me?"

"Let me finish. This isn't some kind of ridiculous half-brained romantic confession, okay? We tried that. Didn't work out. No hard feelings."

"No hard feelings?"

Wow, could he do a worse job at this conversation? He shoved a hand through his hair. No one could make him crazy like this woman. *Still.* How long could someone possibly affect a man? Shouldn't he be immune by now or something? He exhaled, tried again.

"We need to be together all the time." He started again slowly.

"Why exactly?"

"Because I'm keeping you safe."

Raised eyebrows. Tyler couldn't decide if that was better or worse than the verbal darts she'd been shooting a second ago. He figured he may as well keep going, as long as she was going to be quiet for a minute and let him talk. "Noah is in charge here. His police department, his town to protect. He wants my help, which is why I got my police certification in the first place. And he wants me to be with you."

"I guess I assumed it would change from day to day, though, hour to hour…" She trailed off.

"Noah's got enough on his plate. So do his other, regular officers, though I know Clay's planning to help some, too, with protection detail at the lodge. I'm the only one who has a flexible schedule."

"You've got the lodge."

Now it was his turn for raised eyebrows. He was supposed to believe she was concerned about the lodge now?

"So what you meant was…?" Her voice had calmed some as she asked the question.

"All I meant was that we have to spend most of our time together. That decision has been taken out of our hands."

"Whether we wish it had been or not."

"Listen, we have got to put this behind us, Emma."

This time her eyes widened as her brows lifted.

"Put. This. Behind. Us?" She asked the question pointedly and Tyler pulled over to the side of the road, jammed the car into Park and squeezed his eyes shut. Exhaled. Then met her eyes.

"What do you want from me, Emma?"

He watched her consider the question, the car quiet except their breathing and a thousand unsaid words seeming to hang in the air around them. There really was no way to go back to being friends, not with someone who'd once held your entire heart in her hands. No way to be strangers. Except that's what they were now. And Tyler had no idea how to fix it. He'd been trying to, had decided that, for the sake of the case, he needed to show some maturity and just handle the new place they were in by trying to get to know Emma as an adult. Needed to do it not just for the sake of the case, but for Luke.

This wasn't going well.

EIGHT

"Seriously, what do you want? You told me in college that we were through. Not to contact you. I didn't listen. I chased you the way I thought I should. I didn't stop calling, texting—not for months."

He hadn't, it was true. At the time it had only broken Emma's heart more, wondering if she had done the right thing, if she was doing the right thing. The last time she remembered him calling was three months after they'd broken up. She'd been five months pregnant and had felt the baby move the night before.

She'd thought she was getting over him, but after she'd ignored that last call of his, she'd cried every night for a week.

Tyler had tried. Had always tried. It had been her choice and hers alone to cut him out of her life. Their lives. And it was time for her to stop acting like he should have any idea how to handle the situation.

"No, you're right." Emma breathed in, looking up at the ceiling of the car, though no answers were written there against the light-colored fabric. She closed her eyes. *Help me, God. I have no idea how to handle this.* "I don't know what I want."

"I wish I'd known, Emma. I wish you'd wanted to stay with me, that we…"

Were a family? She was guessing, but something about the acute pain in Tyler's eyes made her fill in the rest of his sentence, even if he didn't. She'd known him that well once. Was it possible she still did, at least in some way? "But now…"

And that was the problem, why this entire thing was so complicated. *But now…everything was different.* It was time for her accept that, to let the past be behind them. To move forward. To let Tyler do what he could to keep her safe. To quit acting like she held something against him, because she didn't. Any mistakes they'd made back then, they'd been to blame for equally.

It was time to start as fresh as they could.

"I want us to be friends." She hadn't known that was what she yearned for until it came out of her mouth, but yes, she did want that. Was it awkward, to rip apart the closeness they'd shared, turn into strangers and then try to find some middle ground? Already she'd say yes. But she wanted it nevertheless.

"Okay." His eyes didn't leave hers and Emma swallowed hard. There was a console between them, so much more between them that no one could see, but just in his gaze there was a closeness that surprised her. He might as well have held her hand, or brushed her face with his fingertips. Her breath caught just the same way. She felt tears building in the corners of her eyes as she acknowledged to herself that this was it, this one moment of closeness, vulnerability was a pivotal moment for both of them. After this they'd be friends. Pals. People without a river of history between them. People who may as well have never been in love.

Because one thing Emma now knew, ever since she'd fully embraced God and began to absorb what He'd been teaching her, was that the girl she'd been in college had been selfish. She'd not cared nearly as much about Tyler's dreams as she had her own, even as they'd approached graduation and real life.

That was changing now. And what Tyler cared about was this town, his family, his lodge. She'd seen it all now, understood it. Asking him to give all that up before had been wrong. And she was going to make up for it now by supporting what he wanted as much as possible. He had a life. She didn't fit into it. And she needed to make sure she kept as much emotional distance as possible so neither of them got hurt this time around.

"So." He still hadn't wavered in his eye contact and Emma wanted to memorize the details of the different shades of green in his eyes, didn't want to move. Didn't want reality to stop whatever this overwhelming feeling was.

"So…?"

"We should go…to the lodge," Emma said, hoping she didn't sound as out of breath as she was. Could staring into someone's eyes really disquiet her this much?

"We should."

Like they were suspended in some kind of slow motion, nothing was hurried. Tyler reached for the shifter, put the car back in Drive and pulled back onto the road.

And the weightiness, the heart-pounding, breath-stopping importance was gone. Just that fast.

They were starting over. For their sakes. For Luke's sake. For the sake of finding who was after her and giving both of them their lives back.

Even if Emma wondered now how worth it her life in Dallas was—did she even want to go back? There'd been no one to notify of her plans besides someone at work and at the police department in case they'd needed to reach her. The police she obviously trusted and the person at work was an admin who'd started working there partly on Emma's recommendation—it was the sister of a man she'd dated briefly months ago. Things hadn't worked out with her and Richard, but they'd parted amicably. Like Tyler, he and Emma had just wanted different things out of life. He was a politician, which required a degree of schmoozing Emma could never live again. She'd had enough of that as her high-society parents' only child.

Anyway, besides those two people who she was barely close to enough for it to count, no one in Dallas would even have missed her if she'd just picked up and left. Luke had friends at school who'd miss him, but Emma held most people at arm's length, didn't let people close. Shouldn't she have more connections to show for after living in a city for so many years? If Tyler had ever left Moose Haven, the entire town would have been impacted. Strange, the contrast in their lives.

They pulled up to the lodge minutes later and Emma exhaled. "Is it strange how much this place makes me feel like maybe everything will be okay?" The question was out before she could weigh it or decide if she really wanted to let Tyler know what she was thinking.

But his smile seemed genuine and clear. So maybe it was okay that she'd just articulated the sentiment aloud. "It's that kind of place. Always has been." He opened his door, turned back to her. "Come on, let's go inside and see what else we can figure out."

She wished she had his confidence but it warmed her inside to know that he was so determined to protect her and Luke. She climbed from the car and started across the parking lot, her heart feeling slightly lighter with each step. She still felt like she needed to look over her shoulder all the time, the panic from earlier was still heavy, settled over her, waiting to steal her peace again at any moment, but at least she felt like she was on a team now. Like she wasn't alone. The other Dawsons had rallied around her the minute they'd arrived, something that had surprised her to no end. And now she had Tyler, too. His help, anyway.

She'd just reached the stairs when she heard the first shot exploding in the air and shattering every illusion of peace she'd thought had been real.

She wasn't safe.

"Tyler!" How his name was the first thing she thought to scream, Emma didn't know, but she screamed it as she ran, feet kicking up gravel even as another gunshot and then another hit the gravel too close to her feet.

Dust flew. She heard Tyler yell her name.

Just as she made it to the steps, she tripped, falling hard on her hands and knees, the pain of gravel embedding into her palms barely registering. Who was shooting? Where was Luke…was he safe?

When would this all stop?

Emma struggled to get her bearings, pain coming from too many places in her body for her to be able to think clearly.

And then there were arms around her, pulling her to her feet. "Stay with me, Emma." Not Tyler's voice, she didn't think. Who had her? She blinked, noticing for the first time that her calf was bleeding. From the fall? Had she been shot? It seemed like a lot of blood for a gravel scrape, dampening her jeans in a dark stain below her knee.

She stumbled up the steps, pulled by…she looked up. *Clay?* Where had Tyler gone? The last few minutes had been such a tangle of noise and action she'd lost track of him somehow.

The shots had stopped.

Movement from the corner of her right eye caught her attention. *There* was Tyler, sprinting through the woods after whoever had been shooting.

For a second she really wondered if her heart had stopped. Was he crazy, putting himself in danger like that, confronting someone who was desperate enough to have traveled across the continent just to stop her from…what? Why would someone possibly be this motivated to kill her? She didn't have enemies, didn't have enough involvement anywhere in Dallas to have made them. And she hadn't seen anything when her boss was killed that could incriminate anyone.

Whoever was after her didn't seem to care at all about collateral damage. She didn't get the feeling the killer was trying to hurt any of the Dawsons, but was sure he wouldn't hesitate if it came down to it.

"Come on, Emma. We've got to get you inside."

She swallowed hard, did her best to stay on her feet so Clay wouldn't have to support so much of her weight. Did her best to focus on breathing in and out and not focus on the burning she'd finally started to feel in her leg. Or the burning in her chest she'd had ever since she'd seen Tyler running into the woods.

Finally they were in the lodge and Summer was shutting the heavy door behind them as soon as they were safely inside. "What happened?"

"Summer, where is Luke?"

"Upstairs with Kate, playing chess. He's beating her." She snickered then her face sobered again. "Did the shots just come out of nowhere like it sounded?" Her eyes moved down Emma's leg. "Did you…?"

Emma was vaguely aware of Clay shaking his head. Her hands were shaking. As they settled her into a chair, she had seconds to wonder if she was in shock, having a panic attack or if the blood loss had been worse than she'd thought and then she was fading into sleep…

"Emma. Emma!"

She blinked her eyes, wondering how long she'd been out and if she'd been sleeping or unconscious. Was there a difference? She blinked again, trying to clear the fog from her mind and the sleep from her eyes. Tyler sat on the coffee table directly in front of where Emma was on the couch. "You're okay?"

"I'm fine. Just mad I wasn't fast enough to catch whoever it was. But they left an epic trail that Kate's just about to go find."

"Alone?" Emma felt her heartbeat speed up. Whoever this was, was ruthless. She didn't want anyone hurt because of her. She'd assumed at first that someone wanted her dead because she'd witnessed her boss's death. But lately it had started to feel extremely personal. Like maybe she'd been the target all along.

"Noah's sending an officer to go with me. I'm going to find him or at least something that leads us to him," Kate promised, looking straight at Emma and nodding once. "Today." She shut the door behind her. Hard.

Emma hoped and prayed she did. She didn't know how much longer she could do this.

"Emma, I've got to look at your leg."

"Huh? Why?"

"Because I'm an EMT and I think you might have been shot."

Tyler's voice was calm enough but his breath was still coming fast. How long had she been out? Had he run back inside and immediately come to look at where she'd been injured?

She reached down, pulled up the blanket that was covering her, and rolled her jeans up enough that her left upper calf was exposed. Emma turned her face away when she started seeing blood, felt herself go woozy again.

"Do you always react this way to blood?"

"No, not at all. I raised a boy to seven." She smiled a little. "I'm used to blood."

"You may be reacting to the shock then."

She winced as he put something damp on her leg, but tried to cover her reaction. She'd already seemed weak enough today and now that she was coming out of whatever it was that had come over her, she'd rather not seem weak again.

"You were definitely grazed."

"I got shot?" She widened her eyes, felt her head waver a little again but willed herself to breathe deeply. "Seriously?"

"This is enough. He's getting too close."

Tyler continued cleaning Emma's graze, meeting her eyes as he tended the wound. "Someone is after you."

"I think we already knew that."

While he was glad she wasn't passed out anymore, glad she had enough of a sense of humor left to try at sarcasm, he wasn't satisfied with her answer. It wasn't what he meant. "I mean, *really* after you. This isn't because you witnessed something, Emma. This feels really personal."

"I just realized the same thing." Her expression mirrored what he would guess his own looked like. Serious. Understanding the degree to which the game had changed—the lengths someone would go to in order to harm her. "But I have no idea who would want to." Her shoulders fell.

Tyler looked away, hating how defeated she looked, and focused on the one thing he could fix at the moment. He finished doctoring the graze, which was mild enough that he didn't feel she needed any further medical attention.

Noah came through the door. "What happened? Tell me everything."

"Someone shot at us, what does it look like?"

The look Noah gave Tyler made it clear his brother was less than thrilled with the way he'd talked to him.

"I'm sorry, I'm just angry." He stepped away from Emma as if putting physical distance between them could shield her from his tone, which was obviously not true but it made him feel better anyway. "I don't understand what we're dealing with and nothing in the academy prepared me for this."

"Everything in it did," Noah countered calmly as he took Tyler by the upper arm and led him out of the room. "Clay, stay with Emma, would you?" he said as they left.

"Now tell me why you're really freaked out." Noah leveled him with a look. "Is she getting to you again?"

"She got shot, Noah. She could have died. I could have lost…lost the chance… I'm not ready for her to be gone forever, okay?"

"Wasn't she essentially gone forever before as far as you knew? I mean, you couldn't find her."

"Not. The. Same." Tyler glared at his brother. "And besides, there's Luke. Noah, if she dies…"

"Then you're a full-time dad."

"Right. And I'm excited to be a dad. Can't wait to get to be part of his life. But not like that. It's wrong."

"It feels wrong to you."

"Excuse me?"

Noah shrugged. "I think it's wrong, too. And I don't think it's going to happen. But, Tyler, you're losing it. You're freaking out like you can control this situation somehow if you just put enough emotions into it, and guess what? You can't. That's something they can't teach you at the academy because they aren't faith-based, but if God's Sovereignty isn't real to you yet, hasn't already become clear in your life, this situation is going to make it be."

Tyler had nothing to say to that. His brother had just gone there. Pulled the "God card" and he was right, too. Trouble was, Tyler didn't appreciate his older brother having the tendency to always be right.

Noah shook his head, kept going even without a response. "God brought her back here, Tyler. I don't think He plans for you to lose her yet. But we don't know, okay? And we can't be God. All we can do is the best we can."

"You didn't sound so relaxed about it when it was Summer at risk. Not so easy when it's someone you care about, is it? A sister is different than your brother's ex-girlfriend."

"Sure. She is." Noah's look stayed steady. "But maybe Summer's case taught me something, Tyler. Maybe when everything went down on that mountain, I finally saw that it was ultimately out of my hands. All I could do was the next right thing, my very best at the jobs God has given me to do. At the end of the day, that's all any of us can do."

"Failing here isn't acceptable."

"I'm not asking you to believe it is. I'm just asking you to believe God has your back, okay? Believe that He's still in control and believe that as far as we know, He's still got plans for Emma here." Another one of those looks. "Maybe plans that will surprise us all."

Tyler swallowed hard. "It's not like that."

"You have a kid with her, Tyler, you have to have some kind of feelings for her still."

"I can't…" Tyler fumbled. "I won't let everyone down again. Won't let her down by letting my emotions get involved. I made a mistake in college, okay? I'm glad Luke exists, he seems like an awesome kid, but my mistake is still affecting people. I don't think clearly around her, Noah, surely you see that. I can't be that…"

"Out of control again?"

"Exactly. Yes." He exhaled. Finally his brother understood where he was coming from.

"Listen, that kind of 'out of control,' not so good. That's why we're supposed to be careful with temptation."

"Isn't that what I'm telling you I'm trying to do?"

"Listen. You made a mistake. You learned from it, okay? No one asked you to be perfect, Tyler."

"Everyone asked me to be perfect."

Noah shook his head. "No. Nobody did. You got that all on your own. But this control thing? Emma scares you because of what she makes you feel. That's not all bad. Some of that is just being in love. How many women have you seriously dated since college? Since Emma?"

Neither brother said anything and Tyler knew why. The answer was in the silence. None.

"You're afraid of falling for anyone, dude. And especially of falling for Emma again."

Tyler breathed in and out, heart still pounding from his sprint through the woods, from his proximity to Emma as he'd patched up her leg, from the knowledge she was hurt...all of it. He nodded. "Maybe. I don't know. But it doesn't matter anyway. It wouldn't be good for either of us. I can't let her down again, Noah. I'm not what she needs. Just help me keep her alive, okay?"

"Okay."

Tyler exhaled. "Did you find anything at the library?"

"Maybe. I talked to Mrs. Brown, who did

mention that there were a couple of men she didn't recognize. They came in, browsed, left just a little while after you did."

"Descriptions?"

"Nothing too useful." He shifted his weight. "I also heard from law enforcement in Dallas. The type of weapon used at that murder doesn't match the gun used the other night to attack Emma."

"No huge surprise since this was a rifle. Doesn't mean it's not the same shooter though. Just that they have access to more than one gun."

Noah nodded. "I agree."

"Any word from the troopers on what was found in Emma's car?" Tyler asked.

"Not much, apart from those streaks of paint the other car left on the side. Still haven't identified who it belongs to."

"Any idea on the time frame for that?"

Noah shrugged. "Not at the moment. Usually a week."

"Okay." Tyler nodded. "So what next? Emma and I both think this is personal."

"Not a witness kind of situation?"

Tyler shook his head. "Neither of us thinks that anymore."

"That's a big conjecture to make on a feeling." Noah considered him. Seemed to be weighing how much he should listen to Tyler's instinct. "It changes the scope of the investigation somewhat."

"I know, but I think it's a change that will help us figure out who's behind this a lot faster."

Noah stroked his chin. "So we need to know who her enemies are, things like that."

"I doubt she has any."

"That's not true of anyone, Tyler. Past boyfriends? Anything like that?"

"She hasn't mentioned anyone."

"I'm guessing you didn't ask."

Tyler shrugged.

"Listen, you need to find out some of these things. It affects the investigation."

Noah had a straight face, seemed completely serious and focused on the investigation, but Tyler understood what he was being asked to do. There was no way he could find out the kinds of things Noah said they needed to know if he held himself at arm's length from Emma. "You're sure about this?"

"I really wouldn't ask it of you if it wasn't necessary, Tyler." Noah lowered his voice. "Clay or I or one of my other officers could try. But you'll find out more about her a lot more quickly, give us an idea of some names we could check out."

"All right, if you think it'll help."

Tyler breathed deep, started toward the door then looked back at his brother. "Here goes nothing." He pushed the door open, headed back to Emma.

He could do this. He could stay detached and still get close to her. Right?

She met his eyes. His heart thudded in his chest.

He was going to keep her safe, to the best of his ability. Unfortunately he wasn't sure he could say the same for his heart.

NINE

Emma lay in bed, wide awake, trying to ignore the throbbing sting in her leg and to forget about the way Luke had fallen asleep in Tyler's lap earlier that night.

Luke had been extra cuddly—despite everyone's best efforts, he'd heard the gunshots. It had tested every bit of Emma's skills as a mom to try to figure out how to handle the situation. If she'd had her choice, she'd shelter him completely, keep him in the dark and utter seven-year-old oblivion. But that choice, like so many others, had been taken out of her hands. So she'd handled what she'd needed to handle and prayed God wouldn't let all of this affect him too deeply.

Tyler had been another story altogether. He'd been extra distant, which maybe surprised Emma more than it usually would have because she'd thought they'd settled things in the car and had expected things between them to be less awkward, not more.

But clearly she didn't know how this was supposed to work. If she did, she wouldn't be in half this emotional mess to start with.

She turned over again, burrowing her head deeper into the pillow, pulling the covers up to try to ward off the chills she hadn't quite been able to shake since being shot this afternoon. It was just a graze, but the truth of the wound had been haunting her all day. *Shot. With a bullet.* How had this even happened?

Emma sighed, looked over at Luke, who was sleeping. She climbed slowly out of bed.

"Where are you going?" Kate looked up from the chair where she'd been theoretically sleeping. Emma wasn't one hundred percent certain that the Dawson siblings needed the same amount of sleep as normal humans. Besides some extra tossing and turning when falling asleep and waking easily, she'd slept decently well. Much better than she'd expected when someone wanted her dead. But the siblings seemed to be taking turns keeping watch over her and her sleeping son.

Her and Tyler's son.

She kept moving toward the door, looked

at Kate. "I just need to go for a walk. Clear my head."

Her brows raised. "Don't leave the house."

"The lodge itself?"

"The family section. Stay close." Kate spelled it out. Emma hadn't really needed her to, but she'd been pushing the limits, admittedly. Not that it was smart to do so.

She walked down the stairs, her head feeling so crowded with thoughts she didn't know what to do about it. She couldn't shake the feeling that they could have been so close to catching whoever was behind this today, if only she hadn't panicked at the library. But it hadn't just been feeling watched, it had been the disappointment at realizing her first theory about her boss's murder being connected to her company had been wrong. Not to mention the way her emotions were on edge from working so closely with Tyler. Maybe if she'd been able to keep her cool, stay in her spot at the library just a little longer without tipping off whoever had been watching her…

Emma moved to the living room, thankful the side table by the couch already had a lamp turned on. The dark wasn't her favorite thing at the moment. She settled onto the couch, exhaled.

"Can't sleep?"

She almost jumped off the couch. "Tyler!"

"Sorry." He moved around from the back of the couch. "I didn't mean to startle you. I thought you'd seen me. I was in the kitchen." He shrugged. "I couldn't sleep, either."

"Today was disappointing."

"Because we didn't catch anyone at the library?"

Emma nodded, appreciating that he understood what she'd meant. He'd always been able to understand her so well. "Do you think we would have been able to if I hadn't left so quickly?"

Tyler sat on the other end of the couch, leaving a cushion between them. He shrugged. "I can't really say."

"Make an educated guess."

"Okay, educated guess says…maybe. Eventually either he would have made a move to attack you, or would have become obvious. It's easy to watch a watcher if you know what you're looking for."

"And you do." It was still strange to her that Tyler had police training, but the longer she thought about it, the more sense it made. He was the kind of guy who was honorable, always concerned with duty and doing the right thing.

"Yep. Noah more than me."

"What if...?" Emma tilted her head, kept eye contact with Tyler even as the thought formed in her mind.

"What if what?"

"Tomorrow. Do you think there's a chance we could set up what happened today? Make it so I'm easy to watch and see if anyone tries to get close?"

Tyler rubbed a hand along the stubble on his jaw, winced a little as he shook his head. "I don't know, Emma."

"You don't think it would work? I just thought if I was out in town again, somewhere public, maybe he'd come out of hiding."

"Oh, I think it'll work."

"So what's the problem?" Emma shrugged, leaned forward, feeling more eager about this than any other ideas she'd had for helping with the case.

"The problem is we'd be using you as bait. That's not my favorite plan."

"Do you have a better one?"

His silence more than answered her question.

"Okay, so if you don't have a better plan, then let's try this one."

Tyler watched her for a minute. "You're different than you were."

Emma blinked, shifted in her seat a little, suddenly so aware of his presence, of the careful way he observed her. It was unnerving to be watched that closely, especially by someone who had once known her so well. There was nothing malicious in it, obviously, just something so personal. "How am I different?" She hoped her voice was calm, casual, made it clear she wasn't trying to flirt or anything else, that she just really was curious.

How did he see her now?

"You're more focused. A little more determined maybe."

"I was too big a fan of fun in college." Emma shrugged. "I grew up, Tyler, that's it. Having a kid will do that."

He nodded. "I can see that." A small smile edged across his face. "Do you have pictures of the two of you? Older ones?"

Emma smiled back. "Tons on my phone."

"I want to see."

"It's in my room."

"Go get it."

Emma considered it for a minute, then hurried upstairs and returned with the phone.

"Sure you're not getting sleepy? I've got a lot of pictures."

"I wouldn't miss them."

She kept the smile on her face but swallowed hard. He wouldn't have missed anything about Luke's growing up years if she'd given him the chance not to. But it was too late to beat herself up about that. Moving on. They were moving on.

Although, if she were honest with herself, the full meaning of "moving on," the idea of Tyler getting involved with another woman… she wasn't okay with that. Maybe it was something she should pray about, ask God to help her with.

Relationships—yet another thing she wasn't sure she'd realized she could talk to God about. She hadn't been in church enough in the last eight years since she'd become a Christian. She went every Sunday to take Luke, so he could learn, but was often so intimidated by the idea of going inside herself that she sometimes sat in the car and read her Bible. Maybe it was because of that that she still felt pretty new in her faith, like she was fumbling around trying to learn everything that people like the Dawsons, who were raised that way, probably just took for granted.

She opened the photo app on her phone and started scrolling through pictures, offering explanations. She began with recent pictures. Baseball. Lego camp. Their trip to the beach. The time Luke overflowed the bathtub because he'd been trying to surf. The oldest pictures were last. As she swiped through those she found herself scooting closer to Tyler as they looked through toddler Luke and finally came to the baby pictures.

"He's adorable." Tyler cleared his throat, voice growing thick. "I know I don't know him, Emma. But I love him. I want to be his dad. For real."

She swallowed hard. "I knew you would."

"How are we going to work that out?"

That, she didn't have the answers for. There were no easy ways to make that happen, not in a world where he lived in Alaska and she was in Texas. Emma shrugged slowly. "Can we just take it a day at a time for now, Tyler?"

"I'd like to tell him soon."

"Tell him…" Her voice trailed off. Tell him what? They hadn't worked out a plan yet.

"That I'm his dad. He needs to know."

"He does need to know."

Exhaling roughly, he met her gaze. "Listen, I know it might surprise him and I—"

"Tyler."

"I don't want to overwhelm him."

"Tyler." Emma set her hand on his arm, her heart in her chest beating a little faster at the contact. "He knows. He knows you're his dad."

Tyler stopped. Blinked.

And then, almost before she could react but slow enough that she knew it was coming, Tyler's arms were around her, in a hug that stole her breath away but somehow gave back all the breath she'd been holding for the last eight years. It wasn't a long hug. She could tell that on his part it had only been a friendly gesture, something to convey his excitement, but she knew she'd remember how it felt for the rest of her life.

"Thank you," he said close to her ear as he let her go and moved back to his side of the couch.

Empty space around her made Emma feel like something was missing. Tyler.

She nodded. "You're welcome. He's always known. I never kept you a secret from him. I've always told him you'd be so excited to meet him."

"Wow. Thank you."

She didn't deserve to be thanked. It was the one thing she'd done right. That was all. But now didn't seem the time to discuss that. "Of course. So..." She desperately needed the subject changed. And she needed physical space from Tyler, time to be alone, maybe cry a tear or two in her pillow for what might have been. But first she wanted to see if he was on the same page with her about the case. "Tomorrow?"

"Emma..."

"Please."

"I'll talk to Noah. If he's okay with it, we'll go into town, see if maybe we can get your stalker's attention."

"Thank you." And then her arms were around him. Her hug had been spontaneous, too. She certainly hadn't meant to put herself in such close proximity to him. She let go almost immediately.

He smiled back. "Anytime."

His agreeing to help her? The hug? "I'd better go to sleep," she allowed, knowing full well she wasn't tired in the least, but also knowing this needed to be the end of their conversation for the night. Her mind was spinning worse than it had been when she came down, full now not only of case details but of details from their conversation to analyze later and wonder about. The way they'd each hugged each other so easily…did it mean anything? Nothing at all?

Either way, they were making progress. Moving on.

If only it felt like her heart was in favor of that option as much as her mind was. She stood from the couch, walked away from him again, straight to her room.

She probably wouldn't sleep for hours.

And not just because someone was after her.

Midnight had turned to one o'clock and then two before Tyler went back up the stairs to his room to try to sleep.

God, what is going on?

What he'd felt tonight toward Emma, it was new, which made no sense considering their past. This was different, fresh, innocent.

He'd hugged her on impulse when she'd told him about Luke knowing about him, just thankful and wanting to share the moment with someone he cared about. And somehow that hug had changed things, rewound time. And for the first time since Emma Bass had walked back into his life, Tyler had felt… young. Like someone who might be able to fall in love again.

Unfortunately that hug and then the one

she'd given him after had him second-guessing the crazy scheme she'd been trying to talk him into. Having his arms around her, being reminded just in the slightness of her frame that she was a woman, someone he instinctively wanted to protect, made it harder to consider letting her go through with this plan to try to draw out a stalker.

On one hand, she'd never been shot at with people around unless it was night time. Every other incident had been when the scene was isolated, so he didn't feel she'd necessarily be in danger.

But she might be afraid, and Tyler wanted to protect her even from that.

The stairs creaked.

He looked up and met Summer's eyes. "What are you doing up?"

"Can't sleep."

"It seems to be a theme." He smiled a little. "Want me to make you some tea?"

She shook her head. "No, I'm good. I just thought a change of scenery would be nice, maybe trick my mind into slowing down and letting me sleep."

"Is this hard for you? Having our family involved in another case so soon after what happened to you?"

Summer had almost lost her life after being hunted by a serial killer this past summer. The desperate need for more law enforcement officers during that case had been part of what had prompted Noah to ask Tyler to become law enforcement certified just in case.

She snorted. "Seriously, Tyler? Sometimes you're such a man."

"And that's supposed to mean...?"

Summer sat beside him on the couch. "I'm not having trouble sleeping because of the case."

"Oh."

"Why didn't you tell us about Emma? Tell me?"

He looked down at the floor, understanding so much more than she was asking. Summer, he knew from conversations with her since the attempts on her life this summer, had always felt like the black sheep of the family, after she'd left Moose Haven to run away with another mountain runner. He'd then left her after she'd ended up becoming pregnant, and then she'd suffered a miscarriage that had left her with a mix of sadness and guilt—as though she'd been punished.

"You let me talk, Tyler, and you never once

said, 'Hey, I totally get how you feel, I've made mistakes, too.'"

"It wasn't… I didn't…"

She raised her eyebrows.

"It wasn't just my story to tell, Summer. What if something had happened and we'd gotten back together years ago? I didn't want you guys to think badly of Emma."

A few seconds of empty silence passed. "You think that's why you didn't tell us?"

"I don't know."

"I think it's because you wanted to look perfect."

"Wow, that's pretty harsh."

Summer shook her head. "No, I don't mean it badly. But we all want to look perfect."

"In our family?"

She shook her head again. "I mean, sure, maybe that, too. But Christian culture as a whole. We don't like to admit our weakness. Either we think it makes us look bad or we think it'll encourage others to sin, and you know what? I don't agree. I think if we admitted more often that we're all human, that we all mess up, it might actually help other people."

She'd clearly thought this through and Tyler understood that. She'd worked through a lot in her own personal life this year. Tyler, on the other hand, had tried his best to block Emma and everything about that relationship from his mind.

"You're right. I was protecting myself. My reputation as the one that people could count on to do the right thing." The words fell from his mouth before he'd even finished thinking through it.

"You know, it's between you and God. And maybe Emma. I shouldn't have said anything in the first place."

"I think you needed to. I needed to hear it." And he had, but now his mind was maxed out, couldn't take anything else.

"Okay, well…" Her voice trailed off. "That's not the only reason I wanted to talk to you."

"No?"

"I also wanted to tell you…" She looked away, her face in a frown. "I don't know, the timing isn't good."

"You may as well come out with it, Summer. I can't be worse than what you've already said." He smiled to soften the words.

"In that case, I just wanted you to know that in a weird way, she's perfect for you."

She couldn't have surprised him more if she'd slapped him. Or started drinking coffee, which she hated.

"Did we not just talk about one of the reasons she isn't?"

"Because you made a mistake?"

"Because…" He loved her too much. Because he couldn't think straight. Because he'd never felt that strongly about anyone.

The conversation he'd had with Noah the previous day about his need for control came to mind.

"Just think about it, okay?" His sister held up her hands in surrender, stood and moved back toward the stairs. "I know you have a lot on your mind. But… I just needed to tell you."

"Thanks." He guessed. "I hope you sleep well."

"You, too, Tyler. Love you."

And then she was gone.

He sat for another minute, then went back up the stairs himself, tension starting to ache in his jaw. He looked long and hard at Emma's door as he passed it, thought about the two precious people inside that room, how different his life had been a week ago when they hadn't been in it.

Then he went to his room, climbed into bed and closed his eyes. Tried to sort out his mind.

He had a lot to think about. A son he had to figure out how to be a dad to. A woman he had to try not to fall back in love with. And a killer to help find.

I'm going to need your help, God.

It was his last thought before he drifted off to sleep.

TEN

If what Emma had overheard when she came downstairs that morning was any indication, they were in for an interesting day.

"You want to do *what*?" Noah asked.

"Just go into town, and have you ready to meet us if anything suspicious happens," Tyler replied.

Emma winced. Uh, oh. It didn't seem like her idea was going over too well.

"What are my dad and Uncle Noah fighting about?" Luke asked from beside her. She'd had to clear up the concept of aunts and uncles with him since he didn't have any others and hadn't been initially sure what to call the other adults, but he seemed to understand now.

"They're not fighting, bud. They're just talking."

"If he's busy *talking* how is he going to make me pancakes?"

"I can make them."

"I told you, yours aren't as good." Luke wrinkled his nose. "Sorry, Mom. Dad is the pancake king."

Emma laughed. "Okay, then, we'll ask him if he can make them when he's done talking."

"Are you staying here today?"

"No, I need you to stay with Aunt Summer and Aunt Kate again. Can you do that?"

He shrugged. "I guess. I wish I could play outside, though." His eyes moved to the window. "Can I today?"

Emma shook her head. "Sorry, sweetheart, not yet. There's still someone… Someone is still really angry at me for some reason. I don't want them to try to hurt you."

"No one's going to hurt me. You worry too much." And then he was off, running through the lodge toward the kitchen. Kate waved at her from where Luke stopped, signaling that she had him under control. Flashing her a grateful smile, Emma took a quick detour to the living room, where she'd heard Noah and Tyler talking, to see if she could help convince Noah it was a great idea.

"She wants to help, Noah."

Emma walked up to them, took her stand next to Tyler. "I really do. Please let me do this."

Noah glared at his brother again then directed his glare to her. "This was really your idea?"

"Yes."

He seemed to think about it for a second or two and then finally shrugged, his posture relaxing. "Okay, fine. If it's something you want to do, and if this really isn't anything more than a walk around town..."

"That's all. Really."

"All right. Where are you planning to go?"

Emma looked to Tyler. She hadn't come up with that much of a game plan yet.

"I was thinking about the harbor," Tyler answered.

Noah nodded. "Okay, nice and close to the station. I like it. Call me if you notice anything."

"Got it."

"I've got to head into work. Erynn's already called me this morning."

"Just to chat?" Tyler teased.

Noah's expression stayed straight-faced. "No idea what you're talking about. She called with a question about the case and I can't let her get the idea that she and the troopers are the only ones working this."

"I'm not even going to argue with you."

Noah waved goodbye and headed out.

"What was that about Trooper Cooper?" Emma asked.

Tyler laughed. "She and my brother have made police work a competition. And it finally occurred to me and my siblings that she's perfect for him."

"Does he know that?"

"Nah, he thinks we're all completely crazy. Can't see what's right in front of him."

Was it her imagination or had he looked at her differently when he'd said that?

Emma glanced away, then remembered Luke's request for breakfast. "Luke would love your pancakes, if you don't mind. Mine apparently aren't good enough anymore."

"Everything about you is good enough." He smiled warmly. "You're a great mom, I don't know if I've told you that."

She didn't know what had put Tyler in such a good mood, but it made Emma smile. For half a second she could almost pretend that her life wasn't in danger. Almost. But it was. And they needed to go ahead and get through breakfast so they could move forward with the plan to see if they might be able to make progress.

So she just smiled back. "Thanks." It seemed an inadequate way to express how much she appreciated what he'd said, but somehow Emma thought Tyler got it.

He motioned for her to go first and she started for the kitchen, where she found Luke talking Summer's ear off about some Lego movie.

"That's what we should do for fun today while your mom's busy. We should get into some of the old Legos we have packed up around here," Summer said offhandedly.

Luke's eyes widened and Emma laughed. Summer had no idea what she'd gotten herself into.

"You have *Legos* here? This is the best day ever! Legos and pancakes!" Luke proceeded to dance around the kitchen.

"It's the little things, man." Summer smiled back, then looked at Tyler. "I heard you're making pancakes?"

"Yep and then we have to head out."

"Where—"

Tyler glanced down at Luke, who wasn't paying attention, but still shook his head and mouthed "Later." Emma appreciated him not saying anything in front of Luke. Her little boy had too many case details in his head already and certainly didn't need any more.

It wasn't long before the pancakes were

ready and they sat down to eat, much like yesterday, feeling remarkably like a family. Of
course, part of that was because of the Dawsons themselves. Emma could see why people
liked their lodge. It wasn't just the beautiful
setting, it was the place itself, the way the family made people feel welcomed. Not for the
first time, she understood why Tyler had felt
he'd had to come back here.

"All right, let's go find some Legos," Summer announced when Luke had put away at
least four pancakes. Sometimes Emma was
still surprised at what a boy was capable of
eating.

"Love you, sweetheart." She bent and caught
him in a hug. He squirmed away, laughing,
only to be snatched by Tyler, who hugged him
in a similar way, the motion seeming so familiar even though it was a sight Emma had never
seen before. She smiled, brushed away the tiniest bit of moisture from the corner of her eye.

"That was okay, right?" Tyler asked when
they were alone. Emma looked up at him, realizing by the expression on his face that he was
completely serious. He really wanted to make
sure the hug had been okay with her.

"Okay" seemed so inadequate.

Emma couldn't come close to putting her

emotions into words right now and it wasn't the right time or place anyway. Instead she just nodded and smiled back at Tyler.

"Ready to go wander around town and see if anyone creepy shows up?"

And now he had her laughing. "Seriously, Tyler? You make it sound almost fun."

He shrugged. "There was a time I thought anything could be fun if you were there. Maybe I still do."

Were they really going to spend the day dancing around subjects best left in the past? Emma wasn't sure how much more she could ignore before she started responding. And that would be dangerous for both of them, though mostly for her. She had no illusions that Tyler's heart had gotten involved. He wasn't the type to try to lead a woman on, had always been entirely too respectful for that, but Emma sincerely doubted he knew how the things he kept saying sounded.

Then again, maybe he did and just thought of it as an appropriate way to be friendly. They had to be in close proximity to each other, and while things had changed for the better after their talk yesterday, it seemed in some ways like the progress they were making was just going to lead them back to the same place where Emma was in love with him and they were all wrong for each other.

Because they had been wrong for each other…hadn't they? Or had she just been scared of motherhood, of that responsibility, of making the wrong choice by marrying Tyler, especially when there would be a kid involved and no turning back on that life-altering decision?

"You okay, Emma?"

Okay. There was that word again. And no, she didn't think she was in any way okay and wasn't sure she would be again.

Mostly because Tyler Dawson would always have part of her heart. And she didn't see any good options for dealing with that.

"I'm fine." Everyone knew *fine* was woman code for not fine at all. Except apparently Tyler because he just flashed his devastatingly handsome smile and led her outside to the car.

The drive into Moose Haven seemed to last forever. Tyler didn't know if it was because he was eager to get this over with or because Emma was so quiet. Was she second-guessing their plan the same way he was? Or was something else bothering her? Tyler didn't know, couldn't read her that well anymore. He just knew he was anxious something was going to go wrong and Emma was going to end up hurt.

Tyler glanced in Emma's direction as he came into town, then moved his eyes back to the road and set about focusing on finding a parking spot. She still looked lost in thought.

"What's on your mind?" His breath caught in his throat as soon as the words were out.

"Me?" Emma blinked.

"Since we're the only people in the car, yeah, I was talking to you."

"Right. Of course. I'm, uh, just thinking about today."

"Nervous?"

"Yes. Was this a bad idea? I'm starting to think I'm full of them."

"I think it'll work out."

Emma looked in his direction. "You still didn't say it wasn't a bad idea."

Even without glancing at her, he knew she was teasing. Her voice gave it away. "It's a good idea, Emma. You're brave to be willing to try it." He pulled into a parking lot, looking her way quickly as he did so to gauge her reaction. Was she blushing?

"Thanks, Tyler."

Just the way she said his name was enough to make him want to turn the car around, drive straight back to the lodge and tell Emma she was staying there, in the relative safety it provided, until the killer was caught. He wanted to protect her, always had, but when his heart got involved like this…

He tried to shake the thought. It couldn't be true, right? It had to be just attraction, something simple to get over. Except nothing had been simple between the two of them, not before and certainly not now. Tyler wasn't sure he'd recovered from the last time he'd been in love with her. If he fell for her again…well, there was a good chance he never would get over her.

"You're sure you want to do this?" he asked, trying to keep his voice steady, betray none of his feelings.

"I'm sure."

He studied her for another few seconds, noticed how much her expression had changed, like her eyes had changed. What had done that?

"You seem different." It wasn't the first time he'd noticed in general or even the first time he'd said something, but he'd noticed something different this time. Despite the fact that her life for the last decade couldn't have been easy, and the last few weeks had to have been incredibly difficult, she seemed…softer somehow.

She'd been reaching for the door handle, but she paused, turned back to him. "I should hope so. It's been eight years. Can you imagine if I still acted like the entitled twenty-two-year-old I was?"

"You weren't entitled."

Emma shrugged. "Spoiled, then. I thought everything I wanted would just happen. Sure, I figured I'd have to work for it, but then things would fall into place, you know?"

"You were pretty confident. Independent." Two of the things that had drawn him to her.

"I was."

"You still are. So what's different?"

"I hope it's Jesus, Tyler. I hope that's what you see." The blush on her cheeks deepened a little and she shrugged like she wasn't used to the attention being on her.

"You believe now?"

She nodded. "I do."

It was one of the things that had bothered Tyler the most about their relationship in college. He'd been a Christian and she hadn't been. While he hadn't been walking with God the way he should have been at the time they were dating, he'd still hoped maybe Emma would come to know Jesus. But Tyler had made enough mistakes Emma had been privy to for her to know that Christians weren't perfect, not even close.

Tyler's cheeks burned and he looked down, opened his mouth to apologize, when he realized they'd already covered this and he needed to move on and let it go. *Help me move on, God. Forgive myself like I know You've already forgiven me. And help Emma forgive me, too. Help her with whatever she needs.* "I'm glad."

They sat for a minute, until Emma cleared her throat. Tyler started and she laughed. "Ready to go?" She pushed the door open and then he was following her, just like in college when she'd have a crazy idea and he'd go along with it because when she laughed like that he wasn't going to argue with her.

Tyler reached out a hand. She looked at it, then him.

He lowered his voice. "If you're being watched, I just figured it might help this look like more of a casual stroll and less like we're setting some kind of trap. That's all."

"I hadn't thought about that."

"Well, I have. We need to look relaxed, like we're just out for a walk. Don't look around too much or look like you're waiting for anything, okay?" He stopped just short of saying it should look like a date, because he just couldn't go there, but when Emma nodded slowly and seemed to consider his words, Tyler was pretty sure she'd heard everything he hadn't said, also.

She slipped her hand into his and he wove their fingers together almost without meaning to, muscle memory taking over. He'd almost forgotten how well her hand fit into his.

Emma shivered beside him as they started down the sidewalk. "Are you cold? I can go back and get a jacket," he offered.

"No. I'm…fine."

"What's wrong, really?"

"I'm just getting paranoid. I feel it already, Tyler. That feeling you get when someone is behind you, watching, but you can't see them and the hair on your neck stands up…" She trailed off, shook her head. "But it's too soon. No way is someone watching me that closely."

"They could be."

She punched him on the arm and laughed, and while her laugh had an edge of nervousness, it was still good to hear it. "Thanks for working so hard to make me feel better."

"Anytime." He tightened his grip on her

hand a little, made sure he was looking around and keeping a good eye on their surroundings. The importance of situational awareness in times like these couldn't be overstated. "So are you ready to see my town?"

"Is this the grand tour?" She smiled up at him, the look on her face so sweet and genuine that Tyler could almost forget they were acting. Hadn't he insinuated it needed to look essentially like a date? And she was delivering. So well, he almost wished it were true.

"Well, you've never seen it all, so I think you should."

"Sounds good to me." She squeezed his hand tighter, smiled up at him again, and for a second Tyler would have sworn he couldn't breathe as fully as he'd been able to a minute ago.

He made himself keep walking toward Moose Haven's downtown, where the harbor was, from where they'd parked on the outskirts. The whole town wasn't too long, about a mile, mile and a half, depending on where you considered the "start" of town. And suddenly it didn't seem like it was big enough. He wanted to walk around with her forever, holding her hand, pretending they didn't have the things between them that they did.

He wanted to take her back to the car, find a pastor, marry her right now.

Tyler stopped walking.

Where had that thought even *come* from?

"You all right, Tyler?"

There it was again, the way she said his name. He swallowed hard. "Fine. I'm fine." He kept walking, looking around for anything that appeared suspicious.

He couldn't marry her, couldn't ask her to do something she hadn't wanted to do the last time. And no matter how drawn to her he was, he was still hurt over the last time, not to mention still stinging a little from the loss of his son's first seven years. Forgiving her hadn't made the wariness or the pain go away. Besides, they'd practically been engaged before, they'd nearly had that chance. Tyler didn't really believe in second chances. You lived life the best you could the first time you made choices and that was it. They'd had their chance. He'd messed it up with his impatience and, while both of them had technically been at fault, he had felt it was his responsibility, as the Christian, to be the one to keep their relationship pure. Even though he'd still loved her, had still wanted to marry her, something had changed when they'd made that choice, and things had started to slowly fall apart, even if the big implosion hadn't come until Emma discovered she was pregnant.

This right here, being beside her and feeling like he was thousands of miles away, feeling like he could never be close to her again, feeling like she was just out of his grasp…this was his consequence. He'd told God he was sorry, told Emma. And he'd meant it.

But actions still had consequences.

Exhaling, he cleared his mind then steered Emma down a ramp from the sidewalk so they could cross the street.

"So we're heading to the harbor? I love looking at boats."

"I remember you do."

"That was our first date, right? Wandering around, looking at boats on Tybee Island?"

He nodded and they were both quiet. He was remembering the past, wondering at the fact that eight years later they were doing the same thing. But in Alaska. With Emma's life in danger. And they had a child. Together. Who he hadn't known about.

It was a lot to take in, and right now he couldn't afford to be distracted. He needed to focus all his energy on keeping an eye out for anyone who could possibly pose a threat to Emma.

So far he didn't see anything. The docks were as quiet as he'd expect them to be mid-morning on a fall weekday. Anyone who was going out in the bay or farther into the ocean was out already, for the most part, leaving behind their empty slips. Most would return in the afternoon, before the sun started to set, but not anytime soon.

They walked to the end of one of the docks, then Tyler started to turn around when Emma spoke.

"Tyler?"

"Yes?" She'd turned to face him, moved closer in the process. Only inches separated them and his arms practically ached to reach out and hold her, pull her close to him, but it wasn't his place. Wasn't his right.

"Thank you."

"For what?"

"Taking us in. Loving Luke. Trying to keep me safe."

He tried to look her in the eyes but she wouldn't meet his gaze. She blinked away tears, looking at the boats, the dock, every-where but him, it seemed.

And then she met his eyes, no hesitation. But the expression wasn't what he'd expect from the conversation they were having. Something was wrong. Tyler felt a shiver go up his spine. "What it is, Emma? What's wrong?" He kept his voice low, tried to look around using only his eyes, without turning his head so he didn't tip off anyone who might be paying attention.

Emma shivered. "I feel it again."

"What?"

"Someone's watching me. Behind me. What do you see? Call Noah."

Tyler pulled his phone out, called his brother while he scanned behind her to see if he could catch movement, something, anything that might explain what she was feeling.

Then he hit pay dirt. There, across the water on the other edge of the harbor, was a figure. "Noah, I've got him!"

"Where?"

"Across the water, near docks one to eleven."

"Clay is close to there." Tyler heard his brother radio his fellow officer. "Meet you there."

"Let's go. I don't see a weapon but I'm not taking chances." Tyler grabbed Emma's hand and they ran toward the car. As he ran, he prayed.

God, help them catch him, please. I want this to be over.

ELEVEN

Ten minutes later Emma fumbled with the seat belt buckle as Tyler practically floored it down the Moose Haven Highway and then turned down several side roads she assumed led to the other side of the harbor where he had spotted the figure.

They'd heard nothing from Noah. Emma's heart pounded as she tried to figure out what to think about that. Had they caught the person after her? Were they hurt, had something happened?

Was no news good news?

"Do you think they got him?" she asked Tyler, hating how breathless she sounded, but she was having trouble recovering from their run, from the whole morning really.

"I don't know."

Emma exhaled. She felt like she was constantly hovering on the edge of fight-or-flight and so far "flight" had been her preferred response.

Before this was over, something inside told her, Emma was going to have to fight.

She swallowed hard against that thought. Did she think she'd have to literally fight the bad guy? Surely running was an option right?

Just like she'd run up here to ask Tyler for help. See, that had been the right decision. There was something to be said for fleeing sometimes.

Then again, she might not be in this mess in the first place if she had had the guts to fight for her relationship with Tyler years ago, hadn't let fear and whatever else chase her away from him after college. Maybe running wasn't all it was cracked up to be. Maybe Emma should stay and fight more often.

She stole a glance at Tyler, feeling free to do so since he'd spent what felt like the entire trip to town that morning doing the same to her. She'd pretended not to notice, but she'd wondered more than once what he was looking for. Trying to read her mood? Thinking about them? About the past? What?

Tyler pulled into a parking lot near the bay, jammed the car into Park and then hesitated.

"I have no idea if it's better for you to come or stay."

Emma reached for her door handle. "I'm not staying here alone."

Tyler didn't argue, just grabbed her hand and held it tight. This time, she suspected, it wasn't for show, but a reminder that she was there with him and under his protection.

They hurried toward one of the boats and as they got closer Emma recognized it as the one the person watching her had been standing near. She shivered and then noticed Noah standing next to it.

"Where did Clay go?" Tyler called.

"Courthouse. We saw someone go inside here but we need a warrant to search it."

"How long should that take?"

Noah shrugged. "Depends on whether or not Judge Martin is at home taking an early lunch."

Tyler blew out a frustrated breath and let go of Emma's hand.

"So, what? We just stand here until someone gives us permission?" Emma couldn't contain her frustration anymore. She looked at the boat, expecting to feel afraid but somehow feeling emboldened instead. As though she could storm to the door, throw it open and find out who was behind this like the dramatic unmasking of the bad guy on those old *Scooby Doo* shows Luke liked to watch when they checked them out at the library.

"That's all we can do," Noah said calmly.

She noticed, though, that he had his gun unholstered and at a cocked position in front of him, pointing toward the ground but in a way that he could have it ready quickly if necessary. She relaxed slightly. If whoever was in that boat was after her, she was still likely safe.

Clay returned before too long, warrant in hand.

"Stay out here," Noah said to Tyler and Emma in a tone of voice that brooked no argument.

Emma looked at the boat anyway, considered following for half a second, only to have Tyler grab her hand again. "Stay put."

"But I—"

"Have no business being in there." He shook his head firmly.

They listened as the two officers cleared the boat. Five minutes later, they emerged.

Empty-handed.

"Gone."

"I thought you saw him go in."

"We did."

"So either he went out when someone wasn't looking or they're still in there."

Noah shook his head. "I don't know what to tell you, Tyler. But there's no one on that boat."

Tyler shifted his weight.

"I'll stay with Emma. Go ahead, you're officially a reserve officer in the city's eyes. You can go in."

"Tyler…" Emma's voice trailed off. She really had no reason to not want him to go on the boat. Especially when the other men had said it was empty, but somehow watching them confront possible danger and preparing to watch Tyler confront it was different. She couldn't lose him.

Not that she had him.

But maybe…one day?

Emma's chest squeezed. Was she really letting herself think thoughts like that? Why? Tyler didn't want her, not really. Yes, he'd tried to get in touch with her after she'd run in college, but he hadn't come after her. Maybe he hadn't wanted to push her, or maybe—as she'd thought at the time—he hadn't really wanted to. It was probably just as well anyway—he didn't really know her as well as he thought.

He didn't know the details about her affluent upbringing, which hadn't been fair to keep from him. Someone getting ready to marry someone deserved to have the facts about that person. She hadn't meant to hurt him…she'd just wanted to keep him from being hurt later when she failed at marriage the way she most likely would. All she'd known was her parents' marriage, one carefully crafted for a public image. There was no ill will between her parents, not that she knew of, anyway. It was all very cordial. But Emma had realized once she got to college, once she'd met Tyler, who treated her differently than any boyfriend she'd had in high school, that she'd never seen any affection between them at all.

She wasn't sure there had been any in years.

No, she came from such a different background. Tyler deserved better than her.

He emerged only minutes later, shaking his head. "I don't get it. No one is in there."

"Is there another exit somewhere they could have used to have gotten out?"

"Maybe?" Tyler shook his head.

"I'll go in and process it for evidence." Noah glanced at Emma. "You say with Emma."

"We'll head back to the car. I don't want her out in the open."

"Good plan. I'll meet you guys at the station in about an hour."

The drive to the Moose Haven Police Department took only a few minutes. Emma could feel the tension radiating from Tyler, saw how he kept looking around outside the car, keeping his eyes out for any threats. He was focused and she didn't want to interrupt that by talking, so she didn't. Thankfully Noah arrived a little sooner than they'd expected and before Emma was sure she was ready for it they were sitting inside Noah's office. She'd positioned herself against the back wall, away from the men who were gathered around Noah's desk. After a few minutes of listening she decided she needed to be involved, too, and moved her chair closer. "Find out anything?"

"Noah's looking up the boat's registration right now," Tyler turned to her to say, and Emma blinked at how close their faces were. Somehow she hadn't noticed she'd scooted *quite* that close and wondered if she could subtly scoot back without making it look like she couldn't handle the proximity. Which, of course, she couldn't, but that didn't mean she wanted anyone else to realize that.

"What will that tell us? I mean, obviously who owns it, but will that help?"

"It depends…" Noah looked up from the

computer screen. "Isn't Dallas 24/7 the company where you worked?"

She frowned. "Yes."

"This just got ugly," Tyler muttered. "Because that's who owns the boat."

"I'd say it was already ugly," Clay chimed in.

"Guys. Focus." Noah shook his head then looked at Emma. "Did your boss own a boat?"

"I don't know. Really, I have no idea. I guess he must have and registered it in the company's name, because I certainly can't think of any reason for our company to have had a boat."

"We need to find out if it's been stolen." Noah glanced at his clock. "Still afternoon in Dallas. I should be able to get hold of someone. Why don't you guys head on back to the lodge, get something to eat, and I'll be by in a hour or so to tell you what I've found out."

Emma was already nodding, thankful to get out of the small room and have some time to think. Tyler looked ready to protest, but when he glanced at her he didn't. Interesting. She almost wished she could see herself through his eyes, see what had made him change his mind.

The boat was owned by Dallas 24/7... That thought reverberated in her mind over and over as they walked down the hall toward the front doors of the police building. *Had* her boss been involved in something nefarious as she'd originally thought? But no, she and Tyler hadn't found any evidence of that. And hadn't they decided it had to be more personal with the way someone kept coming after her? It certainly wasn't a professional hit. Not with the way the attempts on her life kept being unsuccessful.

Still, unsuccessful or not, she hated that someone was after her. Who could want another human dead, for any reason? Emma couldn't fathom it.

It had been days since they'd tracked the person after Emma to the marina, days since anything had happened with the case at all. They'd confirmed that the boat was owned by Dallas 24/7 and had been stolen, but law enforcement in Dallas had no leads on that so it hadn't told them much.

Those few days were a welcome break from the case and maddening all at the same time. Tyler chafed against not being able to make any progress toward keeping Emma safe permanently, but it gave him a chance to catch up on work that he'd been neglecting since Emma had showed up and he'd started putting his newly acquired police academy skills to the test. He'd also had a chance to spend some time with Luke. He was a fun kid. Tyler hadn't spent much time around kids and hadn't quite known how to talk to him or what to do with him, but Summer had ordered a huge Lego set and it had been delivered yesterday and Luke had asked Tyler to help with it, so he had. He was starting to feel like a real dad.

"We've got to do something or I'm going to lose it." Emma's voice behind him made him turn around.

"Think of it as an Alaskan vacation."

"Tyler." She shook her head. "It's not funny. I'm not allowed out of the house, neither is Luke, and while he's handling it better than I am, I'm just tired of it."

"I can't control whoever is behind this, Emma."

"No, obviously not." She paced across the living room. "But no one has even talked to me about the case in days. Is it still being worked? Is it cold? What's going on?"

Tyler was already pulling out his phone. He and Noah had talked multiple times about the case, mostly when Emma wasn't there. He didn't know that he could say it was intentional on their part—he certainly wasn't trying to keep anything from her. But yes, it was easier sometimes without her presence because they could just say what they were thinking, not worry about how their speculations or the possible implications of their ideas would impact her. "I'll call him now," he said with no further explanation.

Noah answered on the second ring. "Everything okay?"

"It's fine."

Emma raised her eyebrows and shook her head.

Okay, so she didn't *feel* fine, but Tyler knew what Noah was asking. He shook his head, tried to stay focused on his conversation. "When you get a chance, can you update Emma on the case? She, uh..." A quick glance at Emma, eyebrows still raised sky-high. "She's eager to hear if there's news."

"Sure, I'll come by after lunch. I actually just talked to the police in Dallas and there may be a small break in the case."

"Really?" They could use that kind of Divine intervention right about now.

"Yeah. They're starting to wonder if two people could be working together, especially since the attacks are so varied in their characteristics. But we'll talk later."

"Great, thanks." Tyler hung up, turned to Emma. "Noah will be here soon to give us an update on the case." He didn't add the part about the possibility of two people being involved. It didn't seem like something she needed to know immediately.

Emma nodded, brushed at her face in a way that made him wonder if she'd been crying and he hadn't noticed. "Thanks, Tyler."

Time dragged as they waited for Noah. Tyler wasn't sure what he was supposed to do to encourage Emma, or if he was just supposed to leave her alone.

"Shouldn't you be working?" she finally asked him.

"Excuse me?" He didn't know what was causing her snarkier-than-usual mood this morning, or if he was just supposed to ignore it. But he was about tired of it.

"You've got a lodge to run and I thought I heard you saying something about occupancy being down. We should work on that."

"'We'?"

"I do marketing, Tyler. I'm sure I could come up with an idea or two that could help."

He hesitated, trying to decide if her being at the front desk with him was too much exposure. That was where the computer was with all the lodge pictures, files and documents. After some consideration, he decided the lodge was a controlled enough environment and it would be okay. "All right. Sure, let's go."

He led her out of the family section of the lodge into the main area, where they hadn't spent nearly as much time. He glanced in her direction and was rewarded to see her looking admiringly up at the log ceilings, the tall, stone fireplace. While the furnishings were mostly either things leftover from his parents or pieces Summer had picked out, the lodge was Tyler's responsibility and he still felt some pride in knowing that now Emma had more appreciation for it. It wasn't some run-down place in the wilderness fit only for backpackers and people who liked to "rough it." It was a gorgeous lodge.

"It's beautiful, Tyler."

Not nearly as beautiful as you. Regret knifed through him as he compared his last thoughts to the ones he was having now. The lodge may be beautiful but it wasn't much to show for the last eight years, not really. Had he somehow sacrificed his chance to have a relationship with Emma, to start a family, build his own life, just for a building?

If he had, he certainly hadn't realized it at

the time. In hindsight, yes, Emma had never been excited about Alaska. The unexpected pregnancy may have set everything off, made her desire to run from the life he'd planned more urgent than it had been, but she'd always had legitimate concerns about moving to somewhere she'd never been, at the tip-top corner of the earth. He'd dismissed her concerns, assumed she'd love it once she got there. Even though his attempts to convince her to visit over a break from school had always been met with hesitation on her part.

Tyler should have paid more attention, spent more time helping her see her place at the lodge, how she could love Alaska.

Or…

He walked around to the back of the front desk, the last thought niggling so loudly in his brain that he couldn't ignore it. Or…he could have told Emma he was giving up the lodge, for her.

Another glance in her direction. Would that have made them work? Or would he have resented that decision forever? *Either way, I didn't even ask You, God, and I'm sorry. I tried to handle that entire relationship on my own, assumed I could just ask for Your blessing before we got married as some kind of formality.*

But God didn't work that way, did He? God wanted Tyler's life, his entire life, without consideration or hesitation. No, maybe that wasn't right, either. Tyler knew God wanted his followers to count the cost of following him. But that was different than weighing God's plans against his own when Tyler knew he should know that God's plans were better, even if he didn't understand.

If Tyler had known that, really believed it back in college, how many things would he have done differently?

As he looked at Emma again, he smiled. At least God had saved Emma, helped her find a relationship with Him. That was the one prayer he had uttered a lot in college, desperate for Emma to know God even though Tyler hadn't been fully walking with Him himself at the time.

"You look so lost in thought, I can't decide if I should interrupt you or not." Emma's smile was small, hesitant.

"I was. Lots to think about."

"About the lodge?" Was it his imagination or did her voice waver a little as she met his eyes? She knew, didn't she, that he'd been thinking about her. About *them*.

"Yes." Because that was also true. "About the lodge."

She nodded, took a seat behind the desk like she belonged there. "So tell me about your social media presence. We'll start there and then broaden outward into other areas if we don't see enough reach potential there."

"Social media?"

"Facebook. Instagram. You've heard of them?" She raised her eyebrows.

"I think we have a Facebook page, because people keep tagging us."

"You *think*?" Emma shook her head in exasperation. "Tyler!"

"What?"

"It's like not having a sign out for your business and being surprised no one comes by. All right, log me in."

By the time Noah walked in two hours later, Tyler's stomach was growling. Emma had been so caught up in what she was doing, she hadn't wanted to stop for lunch. And he had to admit he was impressed with all that they'd accomplished together. Moose Haven Lodge's Facebook page had been updated, special deals posted, including a contest to win a free weekend trip if followers shared one of their posts. And they were now the proud subscribers to an Instagram account, which Emma had volunteered Kate for.

"Kate?" he'd asked, barely holding back his laughter.

"Well, sure, she's excellent with a camera and Instagram is basically stories of your lodge told in pictures. She's perfect."

Tyler had noticed Kate had gotten a new camera, some big fancy one, but hadn't known she actually knew how to use it. It seemed like up until now the outdoors for Kate was just a chance to do risky things on mountains and rescue other people from the risky, crazy things they'd done on mountains. Maybe there were things about his youngest sister he didn't know.

"You guys ready to talk about the case?" Noah asked once he'd taken off his jacket. A cold front had moved in the night before and the mild fall they'd been having was finally tipping toward winter, which Tyler knew wasn't far away. He doubted Emma had a jacket with her sufficient for the chilly mornings and made a mental note to ask one of his sisters to pick one up for her in town.

"Just about…" Emma's fingers tapped at the keys and she looked up with a smile, looking younger than she had since she'd come here.

Not that she'd looked old, the years had barely aged her at all and she was as gorgeous as ever. This look had more to do with the expression on her face, the lack of tightness in her jaw. She looked unafraid, for a minute, not worried about the future.

Tyler wanted her to feel that way forever.

"Why don't we go to our living room?" Noah suggested, his voice even. While technically he gave nothing away, Tyler immediately felt the gravity of what he'd learned from his voice. Noah wasn't the serious one in the family—that would be Tyler—except when he was working and had a lead. Then, he was some kind of focused calm that was always a little startling.

They'd just settled into their seats when Noah dropped the bomb.

"There's an employee missing and unaccounted for at Dallas 24/7. Police had reasons unrelated to this case to search his apartment and found weapons, several obtained illegally."

"Is that all that ties him to Emma? His job at Dallas 24/7?" Tyler turned to face her. "It's a pretty big company, right?"

She nodded. "Yes, it is." She shifted her gaze to Noah. "Who's missing?"

"Kirk Moore."

She frowned. "I'm not sure if I know him or not. That doesn't make any sense. Why would someone who doesn't even know me have a reason to want me dead?"

He offered a picture.

She nodded. "I recognize him, yes. But he's not someone I know well so how could we possibly be connected?"

"Unfortunately, it's rare for real motive to be easily established in a good deal of murder cases." Noah shook his head. "A lot of the time victim's families are never given closure, no one ever knows why."

Tyler saw Emma flinch. She'd never been one to accept a lack of answers.

"I need to know why."

"And we'll do our best to figure it out. But first we have to catch this guy." Noah rifled through the briefcase he'd brought in. "I've got a BOLO out for him with every law enforcement agency within two hundred miles."

Tyler snorted. "Which isn't many."

"Hey, the troopers are on it, along with the Moose Haven PD. That's enough that, if I were this guy, I would be seriously regretting I chose to chase my victim up to Alaska."

"Any idea why he's been quiet for the last few days?" It was a question Tyler had hesitated to ask because he didn't want to make Emma any more nervous than she already was. But now that he knew the other shoe was about to drop, and that they were going to be on the defensive again before too long, he would rather be ready for it than not. It seemed like Emma should have the opportunity to be ready for it, too.

"I'm stuck on that part."

"Me, too," Tyler admitted. It had been the question in his mind almost every hour for the past few days. "Why has everything gone so still?"

"Hey, let's just appreciate it while we can." Emma smiled, though it had more of a shadow than it had been five minutes ago. "Now that we know who we're looking for, you guys should be able to catch him, right?"

"Of course," Tyler said confidently.

"I'm going to go upstairs and check on how Luke's doing with Summer. Thanks for the update, Noah. It's almost over. I can feel it." She practically skipped up the stairs.

Tyler turned to meet Noah's eyes. "Any evidence of this guy coming to Moose Haven? Credit card purchases, anything?"

Noah shook his head. "We're chasing a ghost. And we're completely blind."

Tyler's heart sank. Exactly what he'd been afraid of.

TWELVE

Emma didn't know if forced positivity was better than negativity or not, truly, but she'd seen the questions in both Noah's and Tyler's eyes. She'd hoped the fact that Noah had said he'd had a break in the case had meant they'd be honestly closer to finding out who wanted her dead, but it hadn't taken long listening to him to realize the opposite was the case. They had a break, but somehow the situation was almost worse than it was before. Whether it was because they didn't know where the man was or what, Emma wasn't sure. But she wasn't fooled by Tyler's false optimism, though it was nice of him to try for her benefit.

"Thanks again for hanging out with Luke," she said to Summer as she pulled Luke into a hug. "You having fun with the Legos, buddy?"

"Yeah, but I'm ready to play outside." He

looked up at her, all innocent boy. "Is it safe to go out yet?"

She swallowed hard. "Soon, baby. Soon." If they didn't catch the person after her within a week or two, Emma was already tossing around ideas. Could you get into some kind of witness protection program when you hadn't actually been approached by anyone for it? She'd witnessed a crime and while she couldn't be of much use in a testimony, she wondered if she still might qualify. It wasn't as if anyone would suffer if she and Luke disappeared.

Well, no one *would have.* She'd changed that when she'd come here, introduced both of them to the family they'd never had, the family they could have had if she hadn't been so selfish, so scared.

"I have another new set of Legos I found today, though." Summer smiled.

Luke's eyes widened and he squirmed out of Emma's grasp. "Love you, Mom. Take good care of Dad, okay? I think he's a little scared, too."

Emma laughed. "I'll see what I can do." As ridiculous as the idea sounded, she thought about it all the way down the hall, back down the stairs to where she found Tyler sitting alone on the couch. Then the expression on his face made it seem like not such an absurd request on her son's part. Tyler looked more stressed than she'd ever seen him.

"What's up?" she asked, keeping her voice light.

"Can you really ask that?" He laughed, but there was no lightness behind it. Emma swallowed hard against her own fear, against the tight grip of uncertainty that she'd almost gotten used to but never wanted to feel as her default.

"We're going to get him, Tyler."

"I wish I could do more."

"It's not your job."

"I'm trained for it."

Emma shook her head. "No. I mean, yes, I know. You just finished at the academy, but the purpose was always to help your brother out, right? Be an extra set of hands, an extra guy who could keep someone safe, right?"

"Yes."

"So you're doing that now by keeping me safe." She sat beside him, scooted a little closer. "And Noah is going to find the guy. Okay? You focus on me. Um, my safety." Could she not sit in this close proximity to him without saying something stupid?

"Maybe so." He stood and she wondered if it

was because she'd sat so close to him. Would they be doing this forever, dancing around these undeniable feelings that still existed between them? "I've got a lot of work to do today. Starting with the inside of the lodge and then I have to work on a few of the guest cabins later tonight."

"I'd love to help."

"Sure, an extra set of hands would be good." Tyler attempted a small smile. "Besides, as you know, we have to stay close."

Oh, she knew. What kind of joke was it that required her to be in such close proximity to Tyler every single day? Emma didn't know how much longer she could handle this. She was trying to put up a good front, trying to stay positive, but the truth was that her heart couldn't handle this for much longer.

At least working with him today would be better than sitting with him, having time to talk, time to be physically close...

Yeah, anything but that was good.

She followed him up the stairs, helped him check out some of the guest rooms that had problems and needed basic handyman work. "It surprises me that you do this yourself."

Tyler laughed. "Really? I'd think you of all people would assume that here in the boonies in Alaska we do all the work, including stuff like this."

"Hey now."

"No hard feelings, I'm just saying."

"But seriously." Unable to help herself, Emma reached out, put a hand on his arm. "I don't feel that way, Tyler. I was dumb back then, okay? I thought I knew about your life up here, made assumptions, and I never should have. I wish every single day I could go back and change that, but unless you've figured out a way for us to rewrite the past, I can't do that. It's impossible."

"I can't, either." He stood still, locking eyes with her, and Emma quickly looked away. For some reason, Tyler looking right at her, feeling like he might still have the ability to look into her eyes and see her heart, was an unnerving prospect now. She couldn't let him that close.

"Okay, then." She glanced back at him again and nodded. "What's next?"

"The guest cabins. There's a problem with a leaky faucet in one of them. Want to come be my lovely assistant?" He started coughing as he reached for his tools and moved toward the door, where she was already standing, ready to go. "Assistant? I mean?"

His cheeks were red and he was clearly mortified, which somehow lightened the moment for Emma and made her laugh.

"What, I'm not lovely?" She raised her eyebrows, pretended mock indignation. It was amazing how in the space of minutes she could go from feeling so far from Tyler to feeling like they could so easily pick up where they'd left off. Teasing. Maybe flirting.

"Oh, no, very lovely." He laughed and so did she.

Until they weren't laughing. And he was standing close to her, his face inches from hers with enough electricity between them to power the entirety of the town of Moose Haven.

His gaze dropped to her lips, which she subconsciously parted.

"Hey, Tyler, when you check out Cabin 2 could you let me know…" Summer stopped in the hallway. "Oh. Um, sorry. I had a question about the events schedule that's in the drawer in that room, but you know, I can check it another time. By myself. Carry on." She spun on her heel and was gone, but the moment was broken, at least for Emma.

She stepped back, into the hallway where Summer had been, and cleared her throat. "So…the cabin."

"Yeah, let's go get to work on that."

"Definitely."

Emma turned back to face Tyler. "I just realized I have no idea where we're going, so I should probably let you lead."

He laughed. "How about I go first, then, and you just follow me."

Sounded good to her.

They stepped outside onto the deck and Emma immediately shivered and wrapped her arms around herself. "Wow, what happened?"

"The weather changed. Sorry, I should have told you to grab a jacket." Tyler shrugged out of his tan Carhartt jacket and handed it to her.

She slid her arms into it. "Thank you." She looked around the gravel parking lot, which was about half full of cars. "I really hope the social media stuff we did today helps you get even more people here."

"I think it will." Tyler smiled back at her, seeming relieved in her choice of subjects. "Thanks for showing me how to keep it up, too."

"You'll have to let me know if you see impacts from it. Over email or something."

It had been the wrong thing to say. The chemistry of earlier had moved into a comfortable friendship that had now tipped back to some kind of sadness. Emma had killed the mood.

"Yeah. Sure." Tyler stayed close to her, for safety's sake she was sure, but he felt miles away.

When they reached the cabin, situated down a path a little ways from the lodge, Emma was amazed at how secluded it felt even though it wasn't too far.

"How far away are we from the lodge?" she asked Tyler as he stuck his key in the front door to let them in. "I don't measure distance well."

He looked back. "About one hundred yards. When my parents added the cabins, they wanted to give people privacy and seclusion, for either honeymooners or couples with loud children. I think they spaced them just right so that you feel alone but not isolated, you know?"

Emma nodded. They had done a good job for sure.

Tyler pushed open the door and turned on the light immediately, which made the tension that had been building in Emma's shoulders relax somewhat as she stepped in and he closed the door behind her. She felt on edge for the first time in days. Everything had been so quiet, no trouble at all, that she'd gotten some-what complacent inside the lodge. But this was the first time she'd been away from the lodge, or really outside—besides quick trips to the front porch for fresh air—since the incident at the marina, so that probably explained her change of mood.

Didn't it?

"Tyler, I…" She shivered, but at the same time she had nothing in particular to tell him that was bothering her. What? She was afraid? She was nervous? Being away from the lodge made her paranoid?

Emma was starting to be afraid that she'd never be normal again after all this.

"What's wrong?"

She shrugged off the feelings, tried for something resembling a smile. "Nothing. Never mind."

He continued into the cabin, through a cozy living area that Emma paused to admire. It was done in warm colors that reminded her of both fall and Christmas, and the couch looked like place you should curl up with a book. She felt her shoulders relax some. She was needlessly anxious, that was all, and it was hard to be on edge in a place this comfortable-looking.

For half a second she imagined the people

who might have come here. Families—complete with two parents. Young newlyweds, in love and ready to take on the world together. Emma blinked back tears. She'd never fit in either category, and while she planned to give Luke the best childhood she could, take him on more trips now that she'd had this wakeup call, make more memories, it still wasn't the same.

Nothing could make it the same.

"Can you give me a hand, Emma?" Tyler called from the kitchen. She walked in to discover his upper body wedged into the cabinet under the sink as he lay on his back fixing something.

"I'm not sure I'll be much help. Plumbing isn't really my forte." Although she *had* learned how to turn off the water flow to a toilet after a disastrous incident with some Hot Wheels cars when Luke was two. She was still pretty proud of herself for averting major disaster there!

"If you could just hand me the wrench out of my tool box, on the floor there."

"Okay." She reached for it, handed it to Luke and then stood there, listening to the clinking of the tools against the pipes. "Is it working?"

"I think I've almost got it…"

With a whir and a hush, the power flickered. Then went out.

Emma's throat constricted. Surely everything was okay. Her instincts had been wrong, hadn't they? She swallowed hard against the almost palpable lump of fear. "Did you do that?" she asked Tyler, voice at a whisper.

"It's plumbing work, not electrical."

"So that's a no?" Her voice quavered. She'd known when she asked that Tyler had almost certainly not been responsible. But that didn't mean it was whoever was after her. There were plenty of explanations, right? "What do we do?"

"Wait."

"Wait for what?" Emma slid down onto the floor, took a seat next to Tyler, who had squirmed out of the cabinet. His voice was a whisper, also, and she wanted to know if it was from fear, instinct because people are quieter in the dark, or what.

"If the power is out because of wind or something…then it will still be out in a minute and nothing bad will have happened because we waited."

She didn't want to ask the next question. But she had to. "And if it's not because of the wind?" There had been no wind when they'd walked over from the lodge.

"If it's not because of the wind...then waiting a few minutes is the best choice. I don't want us walking through the cabin blind, not knowing where danger is coming from."

Tyler moved a little, something she could hear but not see. The lack of power had plunged them into almost total darkness. The lodge had parking-lot lights, but they were too far away to do much except cast a dim glow. Emma blinked quickly, hoping to accelerate the process of her eyes adjusting. Did it work that way?

"I don't know what to do," Emma whispered, moving closer to him.

"Don't move."

He'd hoped he sounded confident to Emma, but the truth was Tyler wasn't sure what they should do either. He was calling himself all kinds of stupid for bringing Emma away from the lodge when things were still unsettled. Yes, they'd had quiet for days. But neither he nor Noah had taken that to mean that the killer had given up. Her coming with him had seemed like a decent idea at the time. After all, they were still on lodge property, they hadn't planned on being in the cabin long, and no one even knew where they were besides Summer who obviously wasn't a risk for leaking the information.

No, they should have been fine. He'd been careful, not stupid.

But whoever was after her was smarter, more cunning, than they'd initially realized. After the few somewhat sloppy attempts that had been made on her life, they'd clearly started to underestimate the assailant.

Tyler wouldn't make that mistake again. Not if he had a second chance.

God, I know I've said I don't believe in those, second chances, but I could sure use one now.

"Tyler. We can't just hide. We have to do something." Emma's urgent whisper, the reminder that she was counting on him, that inside the lodge his son was counting on him, spurred him into action.

"Okay. *Please, God, help me know what to do.*" Tyler grabbed Emma's hand as he stood and pulled her up with him. "Listen."

"Like I have a choice at the moment." She was out of breath and Tyler had a feeling she was dangerously close to the kind of panic that would put them both in even more danger, paralyze her in place and therefore keep him there, also. They'd be sitting ducks. He couldn't let that happen.

"We're going to go to the back of the cabin. There's a closet back there that connects to the small crawl space underneath the house. There's no way he could know about that."

"Okay. So we'll just hide there?"

That was as far as his plan went. "Yes. For now."

She blew out a breath. "Let's go."

His grip tight on her hand, he led her through the kitchen, down the darkened hallway, listening all the while for any signs someone might be in the cabin with them. He'd known leaving the places they'd already essentially cleared was a risk, but it was one worth taking as far as Tyler was concerned. No risk, no reward. The kitchen was open on two sides, would have been extremely difficult to take cover in if it had come to that.

So far whoever was after Emma had stayed far away, taken shots from cover. But they'd kept missing. Had whoever it was decided he wanted a face-to-face before he killed her, gotten tired of misfiring? Tyler knew from what Emma had told him as well as from the Dallas police that they'd killed her boss at close range, so he wouldn't be too squeamish to do so again. That is, if whoever was after her was the one who killed her boss, and not someone who was just after her personally.

Hence the need to find cover, to get Emma to a place she'd be safe. He'd left out the second part of the plan, where he left her in the crawl space and went to confront whoever was behind this. He'd leave her the gun—she'd told him in college she knew how to shoot, like any good Southern girl, so he knew if someone confronted her she'd be able to defend herself. He'd take his hammer, the hunting knife in his pocket, and do what he had to do if he managed to catch up with whoever was behind this.

God, help us bring him to justice. Emma doesn't deserve this, living like this. Neither does Luke.

Then again, maybe Tyler did. It was contrary to all he really knew of God, deep in his heart, but for a second he wondered. Was this punishment? Bring them into his life just to take them away because of the mistakes he'd made? God didn't work that way.

Did He?

His faith wavered as his heart pounded. "Here it is." He opened the closet doors, relieved they hadn't run into trouble so far.

"Here, take my gun. You know how to use it, right?"

She shook her head. "You keep it. I've only shot a few times."

"I can't leave you unarmed."

"Give me a hammer or something."

Tyler smiled at how her thoughts had so closely mirrored his. "All right." He handed her the heavy tool he'd been carrying, then fumbled for the handle to open the crawl space door and pulled it open.

The musty smell of the crawl space was an odd comfort. Surely if someone had been down there today, recently, it would be slightly more fresh. At least that's what he comforted himself with now, knowing he was about to ask Emma to crawl into the all-encompassing darkness. She had to be safe, she just had to. Whether he deserved it or not. *Please, God.*

"Go ahead," he told her.

"Um, no."

"Emma. It's not really the time to argue, okay? Just trust me."

There was a long, tension-fraught moment of silence before she finally said, "Okay. I trust you." She moved toward the black opening to the crawl space, her feet finding the ladder and she climbed down just a step or two. Tyler was on his hands and knees, inches away from her, the closeness making his heart pound even faster than the current danger. "Come back for me, Tyler, okay?" she whispered in a voice that tugged him closer.

He didn't know if it was the sound of her voice, the fact that he could feel her breath against his cheek, or the fact that once again he wasn't sure what was going to happen, but for a minute Tyler forgot all his arguments, all sense of logic. Her face was inches from his, and before he had thought it through, he pressed a kiss to her cheek. And then her jaw, as if his lips were willing to admit what his heart wasn't yet.

He was still in love with Emma Bass.

She kissed the corner of his mouth, slowly edging over until their lips found each other in the darkness. He kissed her firmly, desperate to make sure she knew how much he cared, needing one last kiss. She kissed him back with the same fervor.

"I'll be back," he whispered as he pulled back.

"Okay." Her whisper was soft and he forced himself to shut the door on the crawl space and walk away.

Wishing he'd had the forethought to put

a penlight in his pocket, Tyler walked back through that room, cleared the other sleeping room. No one was inside the house. He moved to the front door, hesitated. Did he go outside, see what was going on at the breaker panel on the back side of the cabin? Or go back to Emma?

Emma, hands down. He hurried back to the crawl space, pulled the handle.

Nothing.

"Emma?" he called, barely raising his voice to normal speaking volume. Someone could still be inside the house. He'd cleared it the best he could in the dark, but he wouldn't risk anyone's lives on it.

If only their lives *weren't* at risk. Sadly, he hadn't been given a choice about that.

Tyler pulled at the crawl space door again. It was tight—it hadn't been tight like this before.

"Emma!"

Time was running out, he could feel the urgency the situation demanded. Standing there wasn't helping, and she wasn't responding. He needed to be proactive, to do something.

He moved through the dark cabin as quickly as he could, finally remembering just as he got outside that he needed to call Noah.

"Hello?"

"Someone has Emma. Cabin 2 crawl space. Either that or something else is wrong."

"I'm on my way."

Thanks, God.

Tyler pushed the front door open, surprised when it gave easily. He'd half expected to be trapped inside the cabin. Outside, the darkness didn't feel quite as dark, the tiny sliver of moon had finally moved out from behind a cloud, casting more light than it had been able to do in the cabin.

He ran to the back of the cabin, where the breakers were located, and more important, where the cabin was raised off of the ground. If Emma had needed to hide deep inside the crawl space, there was a better chance she'd be able to hear him through the siding here than from where he'd been above the crawl space earlier.

"Emma!" he yelled, no longer caring if whoever was after her was nearby and could hear him.

A smell in the air caught his attention.

Smoke?

"Emma!" He banged on the side of the cabin.

Nothing. Not a sound. Not her voice calling his name back at him. Nothing.

Where was the man responsible for this?

Tyler looked all around, willed himself to notice something out of place, anything.

He pulled out his phone. Texted Kate. Need tracking around Cabin 2. Suspect disappeared. If someone had been there, which Tyler didn't doubt for a moment, Kate would find them.

He banged on the wall again, hand aching, and then ran back to the side of the cabin to the front door. He had to find the source of the flames.

Had to get Emma out of there.

THIRTEEN

The air was damp, musty, and it was so very dark. That was what was getting to Emma the most. Darkness. Everywhere.

And a voice whispering, "Come out, Emma. There's no reason to drag this out anymore."

Emma froze. The voice was male. Not one she recognized. Was this the guy they'd talked about? Kirk Moore?

She moved farther into the darkness, feeling with her hands to avoid running into anything that might make noise and give away her location, though in her mind it was a small blessing he hadn't found her yet just by listening to her heartbeat, which was pounding so loudly, whooshing in her ears, that it seemed like anyone near her would hear it.

She heard a slide racking, the metal-on-metal making her shiver.

"It's going to be quick if you come out. If you don't..."

Emma swallowed hard.

"If you don't, it will be very, very slow. But either way, you'll be dead."

Emma heard him moving around, wondered how big the crawl space was, how much distance separated them. It couldn't be too much, the cabin itself wasn't that big. But she'd managed to find a small space between some kind of appliance—a water filter system, maybe—and some support boards. If he found her hiding spot, it was over.

But if somehow he didn't get close enough... maybe she'd make it out alive.

Emma took a deep breath, let it out as quiet as she could, tried to think of something to take her mind off of her predicament, since she'd done all she could do to stay safe.

All she could think of was that kiss. And the fact that she didn't regret it, not one bit. Regret was such a familiar feeling to her, coupled with guilt, that she honestly couldn't remember too many decisions that weren't accompanied by one or the other. This kiss?

Only good.

If only Emma had much hope that she'd be alive to tell him everything she'd realized, to share with him all the things she should have told him years ago.

God... I'm... I'm sorry. I've told You that before, I know, but You know that, right? Regret is eating me alive.

She tried again to slow her breathing, make as little noise as possible.

And then there was banging, right by her head, and she had to fight not to scream, pushing her hand over her mouth as a physical reminder to not make any bit of noise at all.

"Emma!" She heard Tyler yelling through the wall. Her heart jumped. He was so close. So far.

This was familiar.

She couldn't call out to him, not without giving away where she was, but the desperation in his voice ripped at her heart.

"Emma!"

She forced herself to be still. Wait. Just like Tyler had talked about earlier. Waiting was better.

"Fine." The whisper from somewhere nearby was full of hate. "We can do this the hard way."

She couldn't guess what he meant, but she heard noises, like things shuffling around. Heard a small swooshing of liquid. Not much. A cup full? Sniffed as quietly as possible.

Gasoline?

Then a flicker of orange.

A whoosh. Flames.

"Goodbye, Emma."

She heard the crawl space door creak open, leaned past the water filter just enough to see that the figure leaving, climbing up the ladder.

The door thudded shut.

There had been slightly more gasoline than she'd expected, the spot directly underneath the entrance to the crawl space was engulfed in flames. Three feet wide? Emma didn't know, but she knew she didn't have much time. Thankfully there wasn't anything directly around the flames. She glanced up. Except that ladder and the door, both made of wood, and not terribly far away.

Going out the door obviously wasn't an option. Did she dare try to get Tyler's attention? Whoever was after her would hear and she'd give away her location, but then again, he already knew she was somewhere in the crawl space, and it wasn't likely he would come back down and brave the fire to shoot her.

If she wanted to survive, she had to take the risk.

"Tyler!" Emma pounded frantically on one

of the wooden beams, knowing she did not have any time to waste.

If he heard her, he'd come for her. She knew that much. Emma took one deep breath, two. Fought to figure out what she could do, how she could get out of this.

She looked down at the hammer in her hand, not sure if she was thankful she could see or if she was more terrified since it meant the fire was growing. It didn't matter. She had one shot and she was going to take it. Emma looked back to where the flames were growing near the ladder, taller, wider.

Coming for her.

She hit the wall of the crawl space with the hammer. Nothing. Same problem as trying to bang against it. Emma tore at the insulation, chunks of pink coming off in her hands. She dug her fingernails in deeper, closer to the wall, and pulled hard, realizing as she did so that if the cabin had a cinder-block foundation that made up the crawl space, a little hammer wasn't going to do her any good.

Now would be a really good time to help me, God.

One more sharp tug on the insulation.

Wood. The crawl space frame was made of wood.

Thank You.

Emma hit it with the hammer as hard as she could.

She could feel the fire's heat at her back, edging closer. She didn't want to die, and she especially didn't want to die like this.

Wouldn't. Refused.

She hit the wood again, heard it splinter. Again. Again. Again. A small hole, enough to see the moonlight through it but nowhere near what she'd need to get free.

Time was running out.

Tyler had just gotten to the front door when a figure ran out of it, pushing past him. He stumbled backward, grabbed for the guy but missed. He'd let his guard down for half a second and now he'd gotten away. Then again, he wasn't focused on catching a criminal right now, he was focused only on rescuing Emma.

"Noah, suspect heading your way," Tyler called, raising his voice as the man crashed through the woods trying to avoid the trail. He hurried into the cabin, not wasting any time as he ran for the crawl space access door. He reached for it, felt heat.

The fire was in the crawl space?

Tyler could have hit something. He heard a

thudding sound, like someone was taking their aggression out on…

The crawl space. *Emma.* She must be hitting something. He reached for the door handle, steeling himself against what he was sure would be some intense burns when he stopped short. If he opened that door and gave the crawl space more oxygen, would it cause the fire to flare up?

It was a risk he couldn't take. Tyler couldn't even let his mind go there, couldn't imagine…

He ran from the room, back to the outside, but through the kitchen this time where his toolbox was. He'd given Emma the hammer, which would account for the noise he was hearing, but surely he had something else that might help.

Chisel. A second hammer. Screwdriver.

Tyler stuck his hand into the large tool box, felt around as he racked his brain for what else could be in there.

Something cut his finger. Cordless reciprocating saw. He pulled it out, ran for the back of the house and was immediately able to find where Emma had hammered through the wood and had made a small hole. Everything in the crawl space glowed orange, and while Tyler knew the materials were supposed to be at least somewhat fireproof, he also knew that theoretical guarantees didn't mean Emma was safe.

"Move back!" he yelled as he shoved the saw into the tiny hole. He waited only half a second, to make sure she'd seen the blade and moved out of the way, before he switched it on and made quick work of sawing a person-size hole into the side. Then he reached his hand in, pulled Emma toward him, out of the crawl space, away from the flames.

Sirens approached. Noah must have called the fire department, for which Tyler was thankful. He'd only thought of Emma. Not of the cabin, not of what the damage would mean to the lodge.

He'd only thought of Emma, when it all came down to it, when it came to a choice between the two. There had been no question, not even the start of one.

"You're alive." He pulled her toward him, wrapped his arms tightly around her.

"Where is he?" Her voice was hoarse from the smoke.

"He ran."

"Let's go." She pulled away from him, and he found her hand with his. He wasn't letting go, not now, not anytime soon.

"We can't just go running blind."

"Where did he head, which way did he go? I'm going, Tyler. This is over, tonight. I want him caught. Whatever it takes, if he sees me as bait, anything else, I don't care."

"I'm not letting that happen."

Emma let out a sob. "Don't you understand? I can't do this anymore, Tyler. I. Need. Him. Caught. Now, are you helping me or not?"

He pulled out his phone, called Noah to find out where they were chasing him even as they moved toward his car and he prayed that his brother would catch him without Emma's involvement. Because she might think she couldn't do this anymore, might be impatient, but Tyler would wait as long as it took to catch the guy if there was a way to do it without risking Emma's safety anymore. Because he couldn't do *that* again, especially not on purpose.

"He's headed for Half Mile Lake, that's our best guess."

Half Mile Lake was an easy hike from the cabin, maybe two miles away. Tyler swallowed hard. It was the lake where he'd once pictured marrying Emma. But that didn't matter right now. What mattered now was all the reasons the killer might be heading there. The first half of the trail was in the woods, tangled alders that were the heart of bear territory in the summer and even possibly in the fall. The second half was above the tree line, all exposed, so Tyler suspected if the killer had been camping out up there, it would be in the first half, tucked away where no one was likely to discover his camp.

"Emma wants to come."

"Not a chance."

"She needs him caught, Noah."

"Like I don't know that? Let us handle it, Tyler. Right now you protect Emma."

He disconnected and shook his head. "Noah doesn't want you up there."

"I didn't ask that." She pulled open the car door. "Luke is safe? Inside with Summer?"

Tyler nodded. His sister had sent him a text just moments ago to confirm that.

"Then we're going. Is there a way to get closer by car?" She frowned just as she'd started to get into the seat. "Or do we need to hike?"

"There's a trailhead down the road. It cuts about a mile off the hike."

"Let's go." She shut the door and Tyler climbed in, drove her there without another comment, because while Noah was right that it was his job to protect Emma, Tyler knew he also had to protect her heart, her mind, and she was already going to be suffering because of this trauma for a long time. If Tyler could ease that at all, he wanted to. Needed to.

Noah's cruiser was parked at the trailhead, too, but when they got to the trail itself, there was no sign of whether the assailant had turned left toward the path that led to the lodge, or if he'd gone right. Tyler guessed right.

So did Emma, so that's where they went.

This time she was the one who reached for his hand, wouldn't let it go. Linking his fingers through hers, Tyler thought he felt a blister, probably from whatever she'd done in the crawl space to get free. She was one amazing woman. Tyler needed to tell her that later. Needed to tell her a lot of things, actually. And he would, as soon as possible, the second this guy was in custody.

Noise up ahead made Tyler's shoulders tense more than they already had been. With his free hand, he unholstered his weapon, kept it down, but ready.

Gunshots. And he hadn't fired them.

"Get down!" he shouted at Emma, pulled her down in the relative safety of the alder branches. He holstered his gun again. He couldn't shoot at a target he couldn't see, and he needed both hands free.

God, keep them safe.

His brother was capable, and so were the other officers, but they didn't get shot at often and Tyler didn't like that they were now. He thought of Summer, how she'd just fallen in love with Clay. *Please, God.*

Beside him, Emma was tense but quiet. The tears from earlier seemed to have been only momentary, replaced now by a steely determination that was fiercer than anything he'd seen from her before. For the first time, Tyler realized that the brokenness Emma had fought, what had caused her to run from him, had only made her stronger now that she'd let God heal it. He'd never seen her so brave. So beautiful.

Tyler heard someone cry out. The shooting stopped.

"Stay here," he told Emma. Since the person they were worried about seemed to be up the trail, it was safe to leave her alone and he didn't know what he'd be walking into. He stood and so did she.

"Yeah. Right." She rolled her eyes and followed him up the trail.

There, on the ground not far ahead of them, was a man Tyler didn't recognize. He assumed the suspect, by his black clothing. Clay knelt over him, holding something on what Tyler assumed was a gunshot wound on the attacker's leg.

"This him?" he asked Noah, fighting against his flesh, which wanted to hate this man. Whether it was right or not.

God, I know I don't have to like him, but help me not let hate and bitterness invade me. He'd had enough of that over the years and he wanted to be done with that.

"It's him. Kirk."

"Why do you hate me?" Emma asked. Tyler moved to grab her hand, pull her away from the suspect, but Noah motioned to let her talk. Not protocol, but if his brother was fine with it, Tyler guessed he had to be, too.

"Didn't say I hated you."

"Why did you want me dead?"

Something flickered in the suspect's eyes. Tyler shifted his weight, unhappy with the man's body language. It was cocky, in spite of the pain of the gunshot wound, the knowledge he'd been caught, and that unsettled Tyler.

"You already read my rights to me. I don't have to answer that question." He shrugged.

"You have a partner?" It was Noah's turn.

"And no, you don't have to answer. But things will go a lot more smoothly if you do."

He snorted. "Partner? The work I do, I do alone."

That was enough for Tyler. He exhaled. The man worked alone.

She was safe. This was really over.

"Take her somewhere else," Noah said to Tyler. "Let us get him taken care of. We've got an ambulance coming to meet us."

"You don't need my help?" he asked Clay, who was still handling the wound care.

"I've got it."

Tyler looked at Emma. Decided rather than go back to the lodge, he was going to take a crazy chance.

"Come with me."

She did, with one last look behind at the man who'd wanted to ruin their future. And then she stepped up the trail.

Confidently, Tyler thought.

Finally. They could move forward.

FOURTEEN

Emma couldn't begin to know how to process the last hour or two, but the hike through the woods was a start. She understood why Noah didn't want her there as they finished arresting the suspect and took him to jail or the hospital or wherever he was going. Being there would only add more bad memories, more trauma to work through. At least hiking let her burn off some of that energy.

They hadn't been walking long when the woods gave way to openness, like a field tucked up into the mountains. The moon had come out from behind a cloud, illuminating the ground so well they barely needed a flashlight, though Noah had handed Tyler one on their way past. Was this tundra? Whatever it was, it was stunning, and at the far end of her vision, tucked against a mountain's edge, was a lake that shone silver in the darkness.

"What do you think?" Tyler grinned at her, his face relaxed, like he hadn't just been through what they had.

Then again, didn't people react to things differently? Maybe the fact that the bad guy was caught now made it easy for him to feel better faster. Emma didn't know. Didn't know much of anything right now. She was too overwhelmed.

"It's gorgeous," she answered honestly as they walked closer. The lake up close was an even more brilliant color and she felt her tension ease some, her heartbeat slow. "This is Half Mile Lake? I think I remember you mentioning it when we were in college."

"I'm sure I did. It's one of my favorite spots. It's where..."

His words trailed off and half of Emma felt like she shouldn't ask, shouldn't intrude into his personal life, but then again, hadn't they almost always been such a part of each other's personal lives? Even for the last eight years when they hadn't been in touch, he'd always been there, in the back of her mind, a part of her that she couldn't ignore, couldn't forget.

"Where what?" She didn't know where the boldness for the question came from, but she heard herself asking it, so she must have found it somewhere.

He turned to face her. "It's where I'd thought maybe we'd get married one day. It's where I'd pictured, anyway."

"Oh. Wow." Emma looked at the scene with new eyes, saw it the way Tyler had talked about imagining. If she'd thought she was overwhelmed earlier, having been trapped, almost killed and then suddenly set free from the person who'd been after her... All of that almost paled in comparison to the knowledge that this place meant so much to Tyler. That he'd pictured her becoming his wife here.

Small ripples, too small to really be called waves, lapped the shore and Emma just stared at them, letting Tyler's words sink into her head.

He'd dreamed of taking her to this lake, marrying her here.

"Emma?"

She swung her gaze back in his direction, taking in every detail about him she'd been trying to ignore, for the sake of her heart. They couldn't have a future together. She'd hurt him too badly, didn't deserve his forgiveness. Yet as she let her eyes slowly follow the stubble on his solid jaw, brush over his lips, then move to meet his eyes, she felt her reasons disappearing. Felt everything disappearing except how badly she wanted to bridge the distance between them and kiss him. Not like earlier, when he'd kissed her out of desperation, out of the fear they weren't going to make it out of the situation alive. That kiss had been electric but hasty. Impulsive.

This one was well thought out. For the first time in eight years, intentional. Deliberate. She closed the distance between them.

Her lips found his immediately, the familiarity making it seem like it had been yesterday when they'd been this close emotionally, and as he kissed her back, Emma knew it wasn't just her, knew she wasn't the only one who wanted a second chance. The earlier kiss, before he'd hidden her away in the crawl space, hadn't been a fluke. Wasn't something he regretted as she'd briefly wondered when she'd climbed into the darkness.

He'd meant it.

Second chances…those exist in life? She didn't know, all she knew was his lips on hers, the spinning in her head as she let herself get lost in that moment. This was Tyler, the only man she'd ever really loved, the man who'd maybe known her better than anyone else on the planet did.

But what she'd done to him…not telling him about Luke…

Emma pulled away, ending the kiss.

"Emma?" Tyler's voice was out of breath.

She looked away.

"Emma, look at me."

Her throat felt like it was closing, her eyes gathering tears. "What I did was unforgivable, Tyler."

"What?"

"Leaving. Even if I felt it was best for you at the time, it was still selfish for me to take the decision out of your hands. I didn't explain, I didn't give you a chance, I just left. I didn't tell you about your son for *eight years*, Tyler. You can't just forgive that. We can't start over."

"I can, Emma."

"You can't. I'm sorry, but we can't just pretend it didn't happen. Can't just…do this again." Emma stepped back, tripping over a rock. Tyler reached out, grabbed her arms, but she fought his touch. "I'm serious, Tyler."

"I was trying to help."

"Don't." She spun around, suddenly aware of the vast wilderness around them and feeling more alone than she could remember feeling in her entire life. "Don't help. Just leave me alone, okay?"

She stumbled toward where their car was parked, hoping Noah or Clay or someone was still in the trailhead parking lot. Unease settled in her stomach with every step away from Tyler. After all these days of sticking close to him, counting on him to help keep her safe, it felt counterintuitive to be doing what she was doing. But they'd caught the guy, so she was safe now, right? And not a moment too soon because Tyler had given away his feelings, and so had she, and neither of them could afford to do that. They couldn't feel the way they did and if they somehow *did*, it was wrong and they had to figure out a way to fight it.

Or she could just run again. Like she was doing right now.

Self-doubt called her stupid, told her she was ruining things again, that she couldn't do anything right. But Emma knew they were only half truths. She wasn't stupid, it was the smartest thing she'd done today.

Theirs wasn't the only car parked at the bottom of the trailhead, for which she was beyond thankful. It looked like Clay had left, hopefully with the man who'd been after her, because she recognized Noah standing next to his car.

"Everything okay?" He stood straighter as she came closer. "Did something happen?"

"Nothing…" Emma cleared her throat. "Nothing having to do with the case."

"What do you need?"

"A ride, if you could. I don't… I can't… I'd rather not ride back to the lodge with Tyler."

"What did he do? My brother's not the smartest with women. He's… You're the only one… I mean, he's really only ever dated you."

The sobs Emma had been holding back escaped. She'd dated some before she'd met Tyler. Only a handful of times since, but she couldn't say what Tyler could say. He hadn't been the only one.

Regret tangled with shame inside her.

I'm sorry, God. Can I ever be sorry enough to make it go away? Please?

"Come on. I'll take you back to the lodge." Noah's hand was on her shoulder as he opened the door and eased her inside the passenger seat. Emma kept crying as they left the parking lot, drove toward the lodge.

As they pulled in she took a deep breath, let it out with a shudder and brushed the tears from her cheeks. "Thank you. For the ride. For catching whoever was behind this."

"Of course." Noah turned to her. "Do me a favor and be extra careful the next few days okay?"

"You don't think he was the only one, after all?" Emma frowned. She couldn't be alone with Tyler anymore, couldn't stand being so close to him and knowing she wasn't free to fall back in love with him.

Or to acknowledge that she'd never stopped loving him.

"I don't know. Something about the way that guy talked didn't sit right. I can't explain it."

Emma shivered. "Okay. I'll stay close to the lodge for a few days. And then I'm heading home."

"Dallas?"

She nodded.

"Why?"

Why indeed. There was nothing waiting for her there except their little apartment. Luke had friends at school, but none that he'd mentioned since they'd left, so they weren't people who mattered too much to him. How was she going to move Luke back into that place after he'd experienced all this? Even if he hadn't been allowed outside so far, he'd be playing in lodge's clearing in the woods for the next few days. Seeing this place, knowing Tyler and his siblings had grown up like this, made her want more for her son than she could give him.

But it was the way things were. She couldn't fix the past, couldn't change it.

She just wished the past didn't affect the future to such a huge degree.

Twenty-four hours later and Emma was no closer to feeling the freedom she'd expected to feel now that they'd caught the man who'd been trying to harm her. Too many questions were still unanswered and the distance between herself and Tyler added to his disquiet. Emma wished with everything in her she could erase last night, tell Tyler she *did* need him, in so many more ways than she could express right now, but if there was one thing she knew, it was that there was no going back. The past was always the past and life was always moving forward. Whether you wanted it to or not.

She'd be headed back to Dallas in a week, had just bought her plane tickets this morning and arranged to have a new rental car dropped off at the lodge. The extra time was because she needed some sleep before she was on her own with Luke again. Summer had volunteered to spend more time with Luke so his mother could recover from the last few weeks.

"I'm going to head to town," she told Summer. "If you and Luke are still planning to hike this morning, I'd love to look at some of the shops, maybe find a souvenir or two." The last part didn't bring her the hope that shopping usually would have. Instead she felt...sad. Like this wasn't a place that could be fully remembered by a souvenir. Like this wasn't just a trip. Like she wasn't ready for her time in Moose Haven to end.

Wasn't ready to leave.

Emma swallowed hard, did her best to ignore her feelings as Summer nodded. "Sure, go ahead. We've got a fun day planned, right, bud?"

"Right, Aunt Summer!"

Luke practically beamed. Having grown up as an only child, Emma had always wondered if she was missing something in families who were a little bigger, but now she knew she had been. Since Luke had fully started to understand what aunts and uncles were, and that he had so many who loved him, the confidence he'd had seemed to have grown even more. She wished she hadn't had to fear for her life to get here, but coming to Alaska had been the right step. She didn't regret that.

No, her biggest regrets, besides the ones she'd dealt with from years ago, were of how last night had ended, the things she'd said that couldn't be erased.

Part of her wished she could stay in Alaska, even though things with Tyler had ended badly again. She didn't want to take Luke from the Dawson clan, didn't want Tyler and Luke to have to get to know each other on week-long custody visits. But she didn't think she could live here, in this town with Tyler everywhere, and handle seeing what she'd lost.

"All right, well…" She hesitated by the door in indecision. It had been more than twenty-four hours since they'd taken Kirk to jail, but she wasn't used to the absence of smothering, for lack of a better word. "I guess I'll go?"

"It's weird when it's over, isn't it?" Summer smiled, sympathy in her expression.

"Yeah. It is."

"Remind me sometime to tell you my story." She glanced at Luke. "Now's not the time. But soon. We should talk."

"Sounds good." Emma smiled even as her heart stabbed. Kate and Summer were the closest she'd ever felt to having a sister.

She'd thrown it all away in the words she'd said to Tyler last night. Ruined the last chance they could possibly have had because she was afraid. Fight or flight, she couldn't seem to escape the theme even though the danger had passed, it extended to her personal life, too. And she'd chosen flight. Again. With a last smile at Summer, she gave Luke a hug, then headed down to her car before she could change her mind.

Emma had just reached the bottom of the stairs when she heard Tyler's voice at the front desk. He was making a reservation, she could tell. And not the first one she'd heard this morning, either. It seemed her idea for him to take advantage of social media, to do some giveaways to increase visibility, had worked. It wasn't rocket science, not even close to her best, most organic marketing ideas, but it had worked and she was glad for that. The lodge meant something to Tyler. And she wanted him to have it, wanted him to be happy.

Though the thought of him being happy and finding happiness with another woman made her feel sick to her stomach. Emma hesitated, trying to decide if she could walk by him, talk to him like everything was relatively normal.

No. She wasn't ready for that yet. She moved

to the back door, walked out that way, and then around the lodge to her waiting car.

As she put the car in Reverse, it felt strange to be behind the wheel again after a week of being driven around, but she was glad for it. She'd always been independent to a fault and the week had been a bizarre experience for her in so many ways.

Emma looked one more time at the front door of the lodge. Should she go in, apologize to Tyler, even knowing she'd never be able to erase what she said or make it okay?

She would, Emma decided. Later. She just couldn't right now. First, souvenir shopping.

The drive to Moose Haven went quickly. Emma had one more curve.

A car flew out of nowhere—from a blind driveway, Emma realized too late. She gripped the wheel tightly and braced for impact, which came hard into the passenger-side door. The screech of metal on metal, the loud whoosh and then impact of the airbags...everything on Emma hurt.

And then she closed her eyes and nothing hurt at all.

FIFTEEN

Business was more than booming. Tyler had made so many reservations this morning after Emma's latest social media intervention that they were booked at over eighty percent capacity for the next few months, and this was the off season. Hopefully he'd be able to carry out the things she'd mentioned to him after she was gone—the fall events, Christmas-themed weekends—since that had been what had drawn a lot of the new crowd responsible for the jump in reservations.

He heard sirens and his shoulders immediately tensed. The last time he'd heard sirens Emma had waltzed back into his life and, despite everything he'd said he was going to do, everything he'd intended, he'd fallen for her again. Gotten hurt by her *again*.

Tyler glanced out the window, looked down at his phone, half anticipating Noah's call even though there was a possibility they wouldn't need his help. In fact, Noah probably wouldn't call him today at all after all that had happened the last few days. Tyler was supposed to be sleeping, or some such nonsense. He didn't have time to sit around and rest.

Okay, he had time. But he didn't want all that time for his mind to replay things like last night, time for his mind to replay all his mistakes and missteps, remind him that he might have ruined his second chance with Emma. His chance to have a real family with her and Luke, rather than visits with his son here and there.

His phone rang. Tyler reached for it as his heartbeat thudded in his chest. Everything was fine with Emma this time, he reassured himself. The man who'd been after her was behind bars and this wasn't like the last time he'd gotten a call like this.

"Hello?"

"Tyler." It was Noah's voice. "It's about Emma."

"What? She's here, right? Isn't she?" She was supposed to be fine. Had to be fine.

"She was in a wreck on the way to town. She got T-boned."

"Is she okay?" He was always going to care

this much, wasn't he? Hardly had a choice. Well, maybe he did, but it was one his heart had made a long time ago, if he were honest.

"She's gone missing, Tyler."

He closed his eyes. Slammed down his phone before realizing he'd need it in case she somehow tried to call him, pocketed it and hurried out the front door, straight to his car. He drove to the scene of the wreck at a speed that was far too fast for the roads, then got out of the car and headed straight for his brother, stomach churning at the sight of Emma's beat-up car. Beat-up, *empty* car.

"Tell me what you know."

He was hardy in a position to demand anything of Noah, but it didn't stop him from asking. He felt time pressing against him, the knowledge that they were already behind causing panic to rise inside him.

"First of all, the man we nabbed? Kirk? He isn't the one behind this."

And everything stopped. Tyler. The world. His heart. "Excuse me?"

"He told us the truth, oddly, that he does work alone. When we did some more digging into his background, we found that in addition to being an upstanding citizen who works at Dallas 24/7, he's also a professional hit man."

"What?"

"Yep. Discovered it when the guys in Dallas got into his computer. Bank accounts. Emails. That's the only thing that confirms it, but it's enough evidence. A lot of people are getting justice now that he's behind bars."

As though that made Tyler feel any better right now. "Where. Is. Emma?"

"I'm assuming with the person who really wanted her dead. You know when things changed right after we saw someone hide in that boat, when we wondered if two people were working together?"

"Yeah?"

"Well, in exchange for the tiniest amount of leniency in sentencing, Kirk is singing. Dana Watkins is the one who really wants her dead."

"Watkins…"

"Her brother has been on the news lately, talking about health care. He's a state senator in Texas. People are talking about him running for something on a national level."

"Why does Dana Watkins want Emma dead?" It didn't make sense.

"Apparently, Emma dated her brother. And Dana hates her. That's all he'd say but it's enough to get us a warrant that will enable us to get the rest of what we need to convict."

It was too much information for Tyler at one time. Of course, he should have known she'd dated other men, but knowing it theoretically was one thing. Hearing it for certain was a knife in his chest, one he'd probably need to just get used to.

She'd made it clear last night that they were never going to have a happily-ever-after. Then she'd run down the path without him, back to his brother, apparently, who had taken her home. He'd made the trek to his car in the dark, still not sure what had gone wrong. No, that wasn't true. Emma had told him in no uncertain terms all the things that had gone awry.

Did she regret their entire relationship? Because Tyler didn't. He wished he'd handled their relationship the way he'd been raised. Waited till they were married. All of that.

But he didn't regret having dated Emma, having fallen in love with her, no matter how much loving her was going to hurt him for the rest of his days, when he couldn't have her as his wife.

"Are you going to stand there staring into space or are we going to go save the woman you're in love with?" Noah asked. For someone with so little insight into his own relationships with women, like the lovely Trooper Cooper, Noah sure was bossy when it came to Tyler's.

His brother had a point, though. He needed to get his head in the game. Not that this was a game. It was far more important, the consequences much longer reaching. It wasn't a training exercise at the academy, either. This was real life, and Emma needed him.

"Let's go."

They climbed into Noah's cruiser.

"According to a witness, the car headed into Moose Haven."

"Of course they headed out, only an idiot would head in. The road goes to town and then dead-ends. There's nowhere to run or hide."

"Tyler."

The sternness in Noah's voice caught his attention.

"Listen to me. *Into Moose Haven.*" Noah turned the car that direction. Sure enough, Tyler hadn't been listening.

"Into town?"

"Yes. Either Dana isn't thinking clearly or she's got quite the plan, because it's not the move I would expect."

"What do we know about her?" The classes he'd had on profiling, understanding how criminals worked, came back to him and he found himself feeling ready, actually equipped to handle this, amazingly enough.

"Not a lot." Noah kept driving, past the marina.

"You aren't going to stop at that boat? Could be where she's headed."

Noah shook his head. "I already had one of my guys go check the slip, before I called you."

"Okay, so where?"

"Miller's Point."

Tyler could see the appeal for a criminal. It was isolated—one road in and out, where the person who was there first had the advantage. Yet he still didn't see the reason Noah would presume that's where Dana was going. "Why?"

"Someone called me yesterday. They were picking blueberries out that way and saw signs of a campfire. Whoever stayed there certainly hadn't followed the 'leave no trace' rules, so the berry picker took some pictures. From what I understand, he was planning to post them on social media, hold the person accountable that way."

It was weird to think about sometimes, what the internet had turned into.

"Okay, but then?"

"They found a tent. Snooped around to figure out who it belonged to. Got a name and called me."

"Dana Watkins?"

"Yes. And her name meant nothing to me yesterday. But once I went back in to talk to Kirk today, when he finally agreed to talk and said her name—"

"Why didn't you get someone out there already?" Tyler was kicking himself for the work he'd done at the lodge this morning. Hadn't he said that Emma was more important, hadn't he proved it the other night?

"Tyler. Stop. I know you're upset, but I didn't have the chance. Emma's wreck happened when I was still in the room with Kirk. I had to leave him with Clay and I went straight to the accident once I figured out from the description that it sounded like Emma's car."

His brother was handling this well, Tyler knew. He, on the other hand, was not. They kept driving, the road so much longer than it had seemed any other time. They finally reached the narrow one-way part of the road where one side was a sheer rock face and one side was Seal Bay.

"Almost there." Noah's words seemed intended to reassure Tyler, but nothing was going to do that at this point other than seeing Emma. Unharmed. Alive. "We'll find her."

"I hope so."

"We'll find her," Noah said with even more conviction. "You two will work out whatever this is that's had you both moping and avoiding each other, a feat I applaud, by the way. It's difficult when you're both staying in the same house."

"It's not that easy."

"Sure it is."

"It's too late, Noah." Tyler threw up his hands. "Hopefully not too late to save her. Yeah, no, it's not too late for that. I *won't* accept that. But it's too late for Emma and me."

"As long as she's alive, it's not too late, Tyler."

"You don't understand."

"I think I have enough basic facts that I do. And I think you're not realizing the things God can work out. Look how much He's done for both of you these last eight years. And how she's back in your life. You know about Luke, because of something awful that happened to her. God can even use that. It's not too late, Tyler. Not as long as she's alive."

And suddenly his second chance didn't seem so out of reach, after all. Sure, maybe it was technically. Last night hadn't gone well. Maybe Noah was right, and he could have a third chance and a forth chance and as many chances as he needed to convince Emma they were meant to be together, meant to be a family.

If she was still alive when he found her.

As long as she was alive there was a chance. *God, she has to be. Please.*

"You're right, Noah. If she's alive…it's not too late."

He prayed they got there in time.

Emma opened her eyes to yellow. She winced against it, her head pounding. Eyes closed again, she lifted a hand to her head, rubbed it as she winced. Had something hit her…?

Brakes squealing. Crunching metal. And she remembered. The car wreck. The force the other car had hit her with. It had to have been on purpose. Someone had wanted her to crash.

She struggled to put the pieces together, against her headache, against the fog that seemed to have settled in her mind. They had the guy who had been after her in jail. Had he escaped? No, someone would have told her…

Luke. Was someone with her son? Was he

safe? She'd left him at the lodge, about to go on a hike with Summer. Emma swallowed hard, wishing he were inside. Safe.

All she could do now was pray he was okay. She'd tried so hard to be a good mom and now it was out of her hands.

Keep my son safe, please, God. And help me figure out where I am.

Emma opened her eyes again, trying to ready herself to face whatever was coming. The brightness of the yellow still overwhelmed her, but her eyes adjusted to being open finally and she realized it was a tent. A small, bright yellow tent. She was laying on a sleeping bag.

She was alive. She was thankful, but something about that rubbed her in a strange way...

Emma sat up. It didn't make sense. That was why. After trying for weeks to kill her, after possibly killing someone else, whoever this was wouldn't hesitate to kill her now. So why had he? Head still pounding like nothing she'd felt before, Emma crawled to the tent door, unzipped it, noticing as she did so that her hands were coming away from the fabric somewhat damp.

A cold wave of ocean water lapped toward the tent, splashed against gunmetal gray sand and into the tent. Her eyes widened. The ocean. The tent she was inside was pitched at the water line, water coming closer every second, she realized after watching for thirty seconds or so.

Someone had brought her here intentionally. Left her to die, and planned to let the water dispose of her body. Realization slammed against her as another wave hit the tent. This was sick, awful, brilliant. The ocean would destroy the evidence, and whoever was really behind this would get away. If she hadn't woken up, she'd have been trapped.

Thank You, God. Somehow He hadn't given up on her yet. All these things she'd been through, with all the challenges, He'd been there the entire time, faithful. And He wasn't stopping. If there was one thing she was certain of at the moment, it was that He was even more amazing than she'd realized. He kept offering her grace.

For some reason Tyler's face appeared in her head. Her objections the other night, her insistence it was too late for them…

God kept offering her grace and Emma kept trying to turn it down, kept trying to insist she wasn't good enough. For some reason, here on this beach, probably literal inches from death at this point, she realized as she climbed from the tent, boots getting wet as she did so, everything made perfect sense. She was a beneficiary of God's grace every single day and, no matter what, she was a part of God's family forever through nothing she had done to earn or deserve it.

And every day she accepted the grace it took to know Jesus as her savior…while still somehow trying to insist that she couldn't take the other graces.

It made no sense at all. And explained so much.

God, I'm so sorry. That's no way to treat what You offer. No way to live. Forgive me. A tear spilled from her eye. *I get it now. Grace upon grace, You keep trying to show me. You even brought Tyler and me back together through my desperation when someone was after me. Help me accept that grace, quit trying to earn it.*

She brushed the tear form her eye, stepped back on the beach to put some distance between her and the cold, churning water. And then she lifted her head to look around.

And almost wished she hadn't.

The "beach" was about thirty feet long. And, from where Emma was standing, it looked like there was no way onto it from either side and no way off of it, because the tide was coming in. Emma was between the angry ocean and a cliff that maybe a proficient rock climber could find a hold on, but Emma likely couldn't.

She ran to the cliff first, just to check it out. Realized that even if she could climb up a little, she had no idea how high the water would rise here.

Emma ran left to that end of the beach. Water crashed against the cliff, creating a spray that hit her when she was still five feet away. She ran back the other way, noting as she did that the tent had collapsed and was filling with water with every wave.

Was that evidence? Should she try to save it so if somehow she got out of here, there was something to substantiate her story? Frustrated tears fell but she ignored them and kept trying to figure something out.

God was giving her another chance with Tyler. She'd spent almost a decade refusing to believe there could be such a thing, thinking the sin she'd committed was being punished, thinking the rest of her life lived as a good Christian was her penance. But God didn't work that way. He forgave fully, offered life that was abundant.

And Emma wanted a chance to live it. Really, truly, live it.

She ran back to the cliff, which was now only about ten feet from where the waves were hitting the shore.

How long till they covered where she was standing? Did she have minutes? An hour? She hadn't spent enough time here to know.

Emma put one foot up on a ledge. Tested it for sturdiness and felt for a handhold.

"This is so amusing," a voice called from the top of the cliff, thirty or forty feet up.

Emma slipped, fell to the beach. "Dana?" What was she doing here? Her mind felt trapped in a fog, overwhelmed. "Dana, help me!"

The laughter that came from the top of the cliff sounded nothing like the coworker she'd counted as one of the only people who'd miss her if she left Dallas. Dana had been a friend at Dallas 24/7, had set Emma up with her brother, months ago. Emma and Richard Watkins had gone out once or twice, and while he'd been quite the gentlemen, willing to date a woman with a son, and an overall nice guy, he wasn't for her. Emma had turned him down for the last time about a month ago, when he'd asked her to be his date to some society function.

She'd already lived that life with her parents, had realized even after only talking to him on one or two dates, that she didn't want to do that again. He'd had no hard feelings, wished her the best.

"Help you? Who do you think put you there?"

"You?"

Dana flexed a muscle. "Never miss a day at the gym." From so far away it was hard to tell if she was smirking, but her voice certainly made it sound like she was. "Besides, I did have to drag you."

Emma glanced at the beach, could see the marks that had to have been made by her body being dragged across the sand, at least until they disappeared under the water, which had advanced another foot and covered part of that trail.

Nine feet from the ocean, which Emma knew was cold enough this time of year to kill someone in minutes. In college, Tyler had told her stories of fishermen who'd been experts at what they done and yet still succumbed to the frigid Pacific Ocean when something happened to their boats. It was why so many of them had survival suits when they fished, he'd explained.

What Emma would give for a survival suit right now.

"Why?"

Dana just laughed.

"Dana, I asked you why?"

Seven feet from the water.

"I'm going to die, Dana." Emma wasn't done fighting, but as she said the words they didn't carry the same weight of fear they had a minute ago. She was sad, sure. But for some reason it seemed to make sense to trust the God who'd offered her so many graces. No matter what, He still offered grace. Was still faithful.

She wished she'd figured that out before now.

Emma swallowed hard, willed her tears to stop. She didn't want to die knowing she'd died crying. She wanted to be strong.

"Yes, you are, and I'm going to watch."

"Yeah, I get that." Emma couldn't fathom what was wrong with the woman. "My point is, if I'm going to die anyway, can't you just tell me why? Why are you after me? Why did you kill our boss? I didn't see you. I couldn't identify you. You can help me up, I can walk away. I can't identify you in that crime."

"Yes, but you can in this crime. I'm not

stupid. As for why, I killed Mike because he caught me."

"Caught you…"

"Coming to kill you."

Emma's heart sank.

She had been the first target. Someone was dead…because someone had been after Emma. "Why?"

"You told my brother 'no.'"

"Excuse me?"

"My brother. Richard. You told him 'no' and I didn't like it."

If Emma had had any doubts that Dana was probably certifiably insane, she didn't now. "You want to kill me because I'm not dating your brother?"

"Not just dating him. You're not marrying him. I've heard of your family, Emma. Everybody who's anybody in politics or business has, and their name would have meant a lot to Richard. Could have helped him become president even faster."

President? Richard was one of the best state senators Texas had, in Emma's opinion, but that was a long way from becoming commander in chief. Did he even want to be president or was this another one of his sister's delusions?

"I said no because I didn't feel that way about him, Dana. Refusing to go out with him was the right thing to do. I did it because I cared about him." It was true. She hadn't felt he deserved someone who was settling.

"How could you not want him!" Dana screamed the words, threw something—maybe a rock—that bounced off the cliff near Emma and crashed to the beach.

"Does he know about this?" Emma asked, turning back to glance at the waves.

Four feet from the waves. She could feel the spray against her legs, soaking her blue jeans.

"Of course not. He's perfect. My brother is perfect. He would never do something like this."

"You don't have to do something like this, either. Help me, Dana!"

Another rock. This one grazed Emma's hand.

She cried out.

When she looked up, she saw that Dana—the cause of her predicament and the only current hope she had for rescue, though that had never been a strong hope—had disappeared.

Emma reached up for the rock holds in the cliff again, tried to get a better foothold, then looked up to see if she could actually make the climb.

She couldn't, not higher than a couple of feet.

God, please help me.

Three feet from the ocean.

SIXTEEN

"Do you hear that? Someone's yelling." Tyler picked up his pace to match Noah's, which had sped up when they heard the voices.

"I heard it."

"She hasn't killed her yet. Emma's still alive." Tyler sped up, this time his brother matching his pace.

"I hope so."

"It's true, Noah. Otherwise we wouldn't be hearing talking. Dana would be long gone."

They'd been sprinting down the trailhead since they'd parked the cruiser at Miller's Point. The person who'd called Noah with the tip, it turned out, wouldn't give away exactly where he'd been when he'd stumbled across the tent, because it was a secret berry patch. And while Tyler had suggested Noah call back and toss around the phrase "obstructing justice," his brother had said it was better if they didn't plan to go to that exact spot anyway, just the general area since it was likely Dana would view it as "her" turf.

Just as they'd parked, Noah had gotten a text on his phone from Trooper Erynn Cooper. The DNA they'd recovered from one of the crime scenes and had tested was female.

Now all they had to do was get Dana arrested so hers could be checked for a complete match.

They came to a "T" in the trail.

"Left or right?" Noah asked him.

Tyler appreciated it, the vote of confidence in asking his opinion, the silent acknowledgment that as much as Noah cared, wanted justice, this mattered most to Tyler.

"Left. Toward the cliff." He'd come up here enough as a kid, mostly to try to keep his adventurous siblings, especially his sisters, out of trouble. And even though it had been a few years, Tyler could still remember the view from the top, the cliff face that connected to another trail that was only usable during low tide.

"Noah, do you have a rope?"

"What?"

"In your cruiser," Tyler asked, instinct making his adrenaline pump faster, "do you have a rope?"

"Yes."

"Keep going. I'll find you." Tyler sprinted back down the trail, knowing they were about a quarter mile into the woods and he'd have to make the trip there and back.

He found the rope under Noah's front seat, ran back to where his brother was just approaching the access to the cliff face.

There, at the top of it, was a blonde woman, short hair in a perfect, neat bob. Yelling at someone below.

Exactly what Tyler had thought. If you were trying to get rid of someone here, the little stretch of Miller's Point Beach below was the place to do it. When it was low tide the area had some of the best tide pools and was a gorgeous hike. But you had to consult tide tables, time it right, or you'd end up stranded, watching as the tide came up to cover the entire beach to ten feet up the cliff side.

If Dana had been camping here, watching, she'd know that.

"We have to get to Emma. I think she's down there," he whispered to Noah, not wanting to give away their position.

"We've got to get Dana first. See the gun

on her hip? I don't know why she hasn't shot Emma yet."

"Don't you get it? She's sick. Twisted. Watching her die slowly, now that she's sure she's going to get away with it, is better." Tyler shuddered, remembering again what he'd learned at the academy. Profiling was one lesson he hadn't actually thought he would use, not in Moose Haven even if the occasional crime did happen there.

If he hadn't gone to that class, he might not have thought to get the rope.

Tyler wasn't trying to pat himself on the back, because in all honesty he didn't know where the thought had come from, he only knew that he'd gone to the academy reluctantly.

Now he couldn't help but wonder if God had intended all along for him to learn what he'd learned so he could help protect Emma. Maybe to help save her now?

"We've got to be careful," Noah whispered.

Understatement of the year. At least.

They moved closer.

Tyler had no idea what the plan was.

"We're going to need to split up. Let me take the lead," Noah told him.

Tyler nodded, immediately understanding. "Come at her from two sides."

"Right."

They crept even closer, the soft, moist ground of the forest silent beneath their feet.

Dana was yelling something about how perfect her brother was.

Tyler kept walking after Noah stopped, positioned himself to come at her from the far side, the unexpected one, while Noah took the front, acted as the main law enforcement officer, which he was.

Tyler listened to the ocean, felt the tension build in him with each wave. He hadn't checked the time, didn't know for sure it was even high tide right now, but if his basic theory was right, Dana may have checked the tide, may have timed this perfectly. Then again, she might not have known when she'd have a chance to abduct Emma. It might just be an awful coincidence that the tide could be coming in now.

She was still yelling down. So maybe they still had time.

But not much.

Just when he thought Noah was never going to make a move, he heard him call out.

"Dana Watkins! Moose Haven Police Department. Get your hands up!"

She turned, unholstered her gun and pointed it at Noah. "Don't come any closer."

"You're under arrest for attempted murder." Noah, gun out, took a step toward her. "Don't make it worse by resisting arrest, not to mention another count of attempted murder."

Tyler listened as his brother lowered his voice, softened his tone.

"I said don't come closer!" Dana screamed.

"Listen, you don't need to do this." Noah stepped forward again.

Took another step.

Dana's hands tensed on the gun.

Tyler moved forward slightly, as well. Could he get there fast enough to take her down if he needed to?

A noise at the bottom of the cliff got Dana's attention. It sounded like a rock hitting the cliff, but not like one rolling down. More like someone—Emma—had thrown it. She looked down and in the seconds her attention was distracted, Noah snatched the gun from her grasp.

Her scream was almost primal as she started hitting, kicking, anything she could do to try to take Noah down. Tyler was out of the woods and into the clearing, helping Noah keep hold of her until she was cuffed.

"You've got her?" Tyler asked, slightly out

of breath but desperate to go to the side of the cliff. To see Emma. To see if he'd made it in time. If their second chance was still an option.

"Yes. Get Emma."

"Emma!" Tyler yelled as he ran closer to the edge, slowed down and looked over.

"Tyler, quick! Help!" Her voice was past the point of desperation, and Tyler could see why. She was standing in water, waves hitting her knees, ankles covered in water.

God, help. It was all he could think to pray. He ran back to the woods, chose the sturdiest tree he could find, and anchored the rope around another just to be safe. He wasn't going to lose her now.

Tyler looped himself into a sort of makeshift harness and, with the carabiner in his pocket, would attach himself to the tree to belay her after he gave her the rope. He'd paid attention to Summer and Kate's antics over the years to know that while it wasn't ideal, and a true belay system would be better, it should work.

They could do this.

Tyler ran back to the edge, threw the rope down. "Grab the rope! I'm going to back up and belay you. Count to five to give me time to clip into a rope I've got around a tree, and then go."

"I can't do it, Tyler—and the water is cold. Really cold."

"Emma, you can do this."

"I don't want to die yet. I have Luke... I want to have...you..."

"I heard what you said the other night, Emma, and I'm ignoring all of it, okay? I love you. I think we're supposed to be together. But first we have to get you up this cliff. Come on, you're the woman who broke out of a crawl space with a hammer. You just distracted Dana enough for us to get her. You can do this! Now!"

"Okay, I'm counting, so find that tree and hang on."

He'd just clipped into his rigged system when he felt a tug as Emma trusted the rope to hold her weight. He held tight to the end of the rope in his hands, pulling slightly to help her, amazed at the feeling of the tension and the knowledge that it was Emma.

When was the last time he'd trusted God that way?

Tyler swallowed hard, pulling the rope, fully focused.

He'd held God at arm's length since he'd lost Emma. But God hadn't taken her from him. It had been his own bad choices, a series of unexpected things. God was faithful, worth trusting with all Tyler's weight.

I'm sorry, God. I need to trust more.

Even in God's forgiveness? Tyler didn't know where the thought came from, but that one hit him squarely on the truth he hadn't wanted to acknowledge. He acted like God's forgiveness wasn't complete. Like he still had to pull his own weight. When really he should do what Emma was doing now, grab the rope with both hands and trust that God had him.

Thank You, God. Thanks for showing me. Forgive me for my unbelief. Help me.

"Almost there!" Tyler yelled to Emma, sparing only a glance at Noah where he was still sitting with Dana, who had a look of utter insanity on her face, one that he couldn't have described if he'd tried.

"You've got it," Noah called encouragingly to Tyler or Emma, Tyler wasn't sure.

And then there it was, one hand, Emma's hand, reaching over the ledge. He saw her struggle, but only for a second, and then she was pulling herself up, onto the top of the cliff.

"Tyler." She stood, looked at him for a heartbeat or two, and he didn't want to stop looking at her, didn't want to break eye contact.

He fumbled with the carabiner, the rope, while she made her way to him, slowly. Deliberately.

He walked in her direction, meeting in the middle, wrapped his arms around her and held on as tight as he could. "You're okay."

"You rescued me."

"You threw that rock. So you helped."

Emma looked up at him, smiled, eyes clear. Bright. Like maybe she'd been realizing things on the beach, on the cliff, while he'd been talking to God up here. "Maybe God rescued both of us."

"I'm sure he did." Releasing a jagged breath, he pressed his forehead against hers. Emma was alive. Was here. With him. And Tyler wasn't letting go anytime soon.

Hours had passed and Emma was still cold. She'd had a hot shower, changed into fresh clothes and pulled on a fleece pullover Tyler had bought for her days ago and just never had gotten the chance to give her until now. She looked at her reflection in the mirror in the room she'd been borrowing. She looked so different from the woman who'd come up here two weeks ago. Scared. Full of regret more than hope for the future, guilt rather than confidence.

God had given her hope again. Confidence. And Tyler.

They hadn't had a chance to talk, to really figure out what was going to happen. Clay had arrived at Miller's Point with his patrol car not long after Emma had made it to the top of the ledge and he'd taken Dana to the station. She wasn't talking, wouldn't tell them answers to the questions they'd had. Not about what she'd done with the rental car after she'd hit Emma with it—it had never showed up on any BOLO they'd put out either in the Kenai Peninsula or in Anchorage. Not about how she'd disappeared the day she'd been watching Emma at the dock.

They'd finally learned from Kirk that he'd been hired after that, since Dana was tired of not having any success going after Emma herself. She'd stayed in the area, wanting to keep an eye on things. Once he'd been arrested, she'd taken matters into her own hands again. But, unfortunately, some of their questions weren't going to get answers.

That was fine with Emma. Really, she didn't need answers. She had everything she needed.

Emma took a deep breath, pushed a stand of errant hair behind her ear, put on a little lip gloss.

She'd just started down the stairs when Luke ran up them. "Mom!" He threw his arms around her. "You're really okay?"

They'd left out every detail possible this week, so all he knew was that she'd gotten a little hurt a couple of times when the bad guys had tried to get her. It was really all that a boy his age needed to know. More than, really. She wanted to protect his innocence as long as possible.

"I'm okay, sweetheart. I was just a little cold from being in the ocean."

He hugged her tight. Looked up at her. "One day, when I'm older, will you tell me what really happened?"

"Yes. I will."

Satisfied, he nodded, started to push past her to get up the stairs. Emma guessed to get the baseball glove and ball Tyler had surprised him with when they'd gotten back to the lodge that morning after the rescue and arrest.

"You going outside to play?" she asked him, loving the idea of her son getting to run around again. To be free.

Emma wondered if God ever felt that way, pleased when His children enjoyed the freedom and abundant life He'd given them. It was an interesting thought she'd have to think about more later.

"Yep! Dad's going to come out and play with me."

"He'll be out in a minute, okay, Luke? I've got to talk to him really quickly." What she had to say wouldn't take long. Just that she loved him. Didn't want to go back to Texas. Wanted to live happily ever after with him. Easy stuff.

"Okay." He hurried up the stairs, paused at the top and looked back at her. "You look pretty, Mom. Really pretty. Even with that weird stuff on your lips."

Emma laughed as he disappeared down the hallway in search of the glove.

"He's right, you know." She heard Tyler's voice from the bottom of the stairs. And while she wouldn't have thought it possible, her heart skipped a beat, like she was some teenager who'd just fallen in love instead of a grown woman with a son who had spent the last eight years of her life thinking she'd be alone forever. Thinking she *deserved* to be.

God, thank You for showing me.

"He's right, huh?" Emma started down the stairs. "So the stuff on my lips *is* weird?"

Tyler's grin spread across his face. "Not weird at all. Not in the least."

Emma liked seeing him smile. He looked happier now than she could remember. Maybe happier than she'd ever seen him.

He reached out for her hand as she approached the bottom of the stairs and Emma let him take it.

"Hi," she said, feeling suddenly shy, butterflies dancing around in her middle.

"Hi."

"Hi!" Luke yelled as he pushed past Emma and Tyler both, on his way outside. "See you in a minute, Dad!"

Emma was laughing too hard to tell him he should be more careful on the stairs. Her heart felt full, overwhelmed in a good way, completely amazed that in such a short time they'd gone from being a family where she felt like a piece was missing, where she felt like *Tyler* was missing, to having everything she could have possibly dreamed of.

"So I was thinking…" Tyler began.

"Yeah?" Emma looked up at him, loving the chance to just look at him, at the way the years had aged his face in a way that had only made him more handsome than the college guy she'd known. He was a man now, shoulders broader. Jaw firmer.

He was the most attractive man she'd ever

seen. And even if he hadn't been, she was head over heels in love with him.

"Maybe we don't have to start over."

"No?"

Tyler shook his head, smiled slowly. "Maybe, instead, we can start again." He stuck out a hand. "I'm Tyler Dawson."

She quirked an eyebrow. "Emma Bass."

"Nice to meet you." He waited one heartbeat, two. And then lowered himself to his knee. "As long as we're starting again, maybe we could just cut to the chase. Will you marry me, Emma? Be my wife?"

"Nothing would make me happier."

He stood, leaned forward and brushed the smallest of kisses across her lips. "Here's to starting again."

Emma met his eyes, smiled at him and returned a feather-light kiss to his cheek.

Then his lips met hers. It was nothing like the desperate kiss in the crawl space, didn't have the passionate heat of the kiss the night they'd hiked to the lake in the dark.

His lips were tender on hers, gentle, tentative, as though they hadn't kissed countless times. As though there wasn't a past between them.

As though they were starting again. Just like Tyler had said.

"Any chance you want to go see if my pastor is free this afternoon?" Tyler said between soft kisses.

"I can't think of anything that sounds better."

Two hours later they'd told Tyler's family, who was ecstatic. Told Luke, who'd said, "Awesome!" and then gone back to throwing his baseball before stopping, looking back at Tyler and yelling, "Wait. We get to live here with you forever!" And then he'd run and thrown his arms around him.

Tyler looked at Emma, who nodded. Somehow while he'd asked her to marry him, they hadn't managed to talk about their living situation.

"If you care about Dallas…" Tyler's voice trailed off, but she knew he meant it. Knew he wasn't going to let her go this time.

"I want to be here, with you, helping with the lodge." Emma smiled. "Maybe showing you how to use the internet some more to get the word out," she teased.

He smiled back.

Now she was standing near Half Mile Lake, having made the hike in regular clothes and then changed into a wedding dress in a pop-up shelter Summer and Kate had set up—the Dawson sisters thought of everything in a way that would never stop impressing Emma.

Her dress was white, with just enough lace on her shoulders and collarbones to remind her of the Duchess of Cambridge's wedding dress, but with a practical length skirt, with only the slightest train. She was in the pop-up shelter still, having been instructed by her soon-to-be sisters-in-law to stay there until they were ready for her.

Noah had agreed to give her away. Emma planned to reach out to her parents, let them know she'd married Tyler, but since they hadn't wanted to be involved in her life up to this point, she didn't know if she should expect that to change or not. For now she was fine with the fact that the people who had embraced her, welcomed her into their family when they'd barely known her, had without hesitation put their lives at risk for her, were the ones standing beside her today.

Kate poked her head into the tent. "You ready? You look gorgeous. Tyler's going to have trouble focusing enough to repeat the vows." She laughed.

"I hope he can manage to stumble through

them at least. We've waited a long time for this, to be a family. Honestly, I'd given up waiting."

"Funny how God can work things out sometimes, isn't it?" Kate smiled. "Let's go, Emma."

She stepped out of the tent, smiled immediately at the sight before her. The lake, which was even more beautiful in the daylight, was such a bright blue it looked like something out of her imagination. Beside it stood Tyler, the only man she'd ever truly loved, and beside him was Luke, looking adorable dressed as the best man. The rest of Tyler's siblings were gathered around, as was Clay. He and Summer were planning to get married sometime in the next couple of months.

Noah walked her down the "aisle," toward Tyler, whose eyes never left hers. And when she reached him, he took both her hands in his, lifted the left one to his lips and kissed it.

"I love you," he mouthed as the pastor spoke.

"I love you, too," she mouthed back and then listened as the man beside them talked about love, God's design of marriage. She dreamed about what it was going to be like to spend the rest of her life with Tyler and their son. Together as a family.

"You may kiss your bride, Tyler."

And oh, did he kiss her.

Emma finally pulled back, smiling. "Married. Can you believe it?"

"I love you, Emma Dawson."

"I love you, Tyler. Forever."

And she sealed her promise with another kiss. And another.

"Aw, man, again?" Luke mumbled from where he stood. They all laughed, and Emma and Tyler pulled Luke in for a family hug as she thanked God once again for giving her more than she could have ever thought to ask for.

Some stories, she was surprised to find out, really did have a happily-ever-after.

* * * * *

*Go back and check out
the first Dawson family adventure in the
beautiful Alaskan wilderness:*

*MOUNTAIN REFUGE
Find this and other great reads at
www.LoveInspired.com*

Dear Reader,

Thanks for reading Emma and Tyler's story! I enjoyed being back at Moose Haven Lodge and getting to share my favorite state, Alaska, with you again through fiction!

Emma and Tyler were a unique set of characters for me to write, especially because of their past relationship. It was amazing as I tried to get into their heads to see the struggles they would have gone through, and how deep the wounds they'd inflicted on each other were, to realize how much many people may feel like the two of them did. Though it was difficult in some ways, I enjoyed writing their story, and loved seeing how through fiction God reminded me about second chances and forgiveness. If you identified with either of the characters or their struggle, I hope God uses this book to speak to you about forgiveness, as well, and reminds you of his grace.

As always, I love to hear from readers! You can find me on facebook.com/sarahvarland-author, where I post writing news and lots of Alaska photos, or you can email me at sarah-varland@gmail.com.

P.S. If you're ever planning a trip to Alaska,

let me know! I love helping people come up with ideas for things to visit as it's a huge state and there's always something new to see. Hint: if you come visit, you can see the town I got some of my inspiration for Moose Haven from, though Moose Haven is a fictional town located on the Kenai Peninsula near some real towns I may reference in my stories. For now, you could google Seward, Alaska, for a small glimpse of this area and my inspiration.

Thanks again for reading!
Sarah Varland

Get 4 FREE REWARDS!

We'll send you 2 FREE Books plus 2 FREE Mystery Gifts.

Love Inspired® books feature contemporary inspirational romances with Christian characters facing the challenges of life and love.

FREE Value Over $20

Get 4 FREE REWARDS!

We'll send you 2 FREE Books plus 2 FREE Mystery Gifts.

Harlequin® Heartwarming™ Larger-Print books feature traditional values of home, family, community and most of all—love.

FREE Value Over $20

HOME on the RANCH

YES! Please send me the **Home on the Ranch Collection** in Larger Print. This collection begins with 3 FREE books and 2 FREE gifts in the first shipment. Along with my 3 free books, I'll also get the next 4 books from the Home on the Ranch Collection, in LARGER PRINT, which I may either return and owe nothing, or keep for the low price of $5.24 U.S./ $5.89 CDN each plus $2.99 for shipping and handling per shipment*. If I decide to continue, about once a month for 8 months I will get 6 or 7 more books, but will only need to pay for 4. That means 2 or 3 books in every shipment will be FREE! If I decide to keep the entire collection, I'll have paid for only 32 books because 19 books are FREE! I understand that accepting the 3 free books and gifts places me under no obligation to buy anything. I can always return a shipment and cancel at any time. My free books and gifts are mine to keep no matter what I decide.

268 HCN 3760 468 HCN 3760

Name	(PLEASE PRINT)	
Address		Apt. #
City	State/Prov.	Zip/Postal Code

Signature (if under 18, a parent or guardian must sign)

Mail to the **Reader Service:**
IN U.S.A.: P.O. Box 1867, Buffalo, NY. 14240-1867
IN CANADA: P.O. Box 609, Fort Erie, Ontario L2A 5X3

HRCBPA18

READERSERVICE.COM

Manage your account online!

- Review your order history
- Manage your payments
- Update your address

*We've designed the
Reader Service website
just for you.*

Enjoy all the features!

- Discover new series available to you, and read excerpts from any series.
- Respond to mailings and special monthly offers.
- Browse the Bonus Bucks catalog and online-only exculsives.
- Share your feedback.

Visit us at:
ReaderService.com

RS16R